FATE OF RAVENS

Other books by Tiina Nunnally

Fiction

Maija, a novel
Runemaker, a Margit Andersson mystery

Selected Translations

Kristin Lavransdatter 1: The Wreath by Sigrid Undset
Niels Lyhne by Jens Peter Jacobsen
Mogens & Other Stories by Jens Peter Jacobsen
Night Roamers & Other Stories by Knut Hamsun
Katinka by Herman Bang
Laterna Magica by William Heinesen
The Faces by Tove Ditlevsen
Early Spring by Tove Ditlevsen

Tiina Nunnally

Fate of Ravens

A Margit Andersson Mystery

FJORD SUSPENSE NO. 2

Fjord Press
Seattle

Published and distributed by:
Fjord Press
PO Box 16349
Seattle, WA 98116
tel (206) 935-7376 / fax (206) 938-1991
fjord@halcyon.com   www.fjordpress.com/fjord

Editor: Steven T. Murray
Design & typography: Fjord Press
Cover design & illustrations: Jane Fleming
Printed on alkaline paper by Versa Press, East Peoria, Illinois

Library of Congress Cataloging in Publication Data:
Nunnally, Tiina, 1952–
     Fate of Ravens : a Margit Andersson mystery / Tiina Nunnally. —
1st ed.
          p.   cm. — (Fjord suspense ; no. 2)
     ISBN 0-940242-80-X (trade pbk. : alk. paper)
     I. Title. II. Series.
PS3564.U53F38   1998
813'.54—dc21   98-6627
                                                         CIP

Printed in the United States of America
First edition, 1998

For Susan,
with gratitude

FATE OF RAVENS

The matter that detains us now may seem,
To many, neither dignified enough
Nor arduous, yet will not be scorned by them,
Who, looking inward, have observed the ties
That bind the perishable hours of life
Each to the other, and the curious props
By which the world of memory and thought
Exists and is sustained.

— William Wordsworth
The Prelude, Book VII (1850)

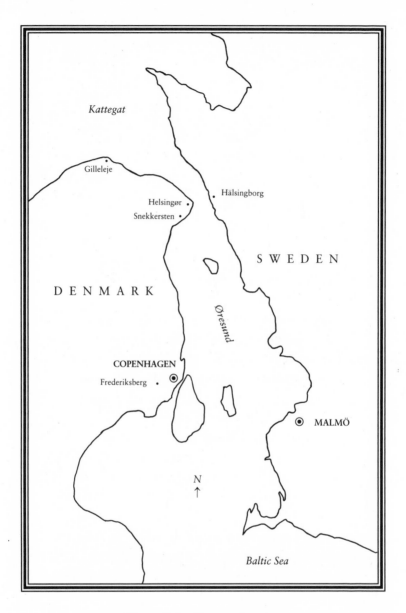

Map of the Øresund region

1

On the morning of July 10th, Rosa Nørgaard stepped out onto the landing and pulled shut the door to her apartment. She was wearing her best blue silk dress and a long brown coat. Copenhagen was in the middle of a heat wave, and the temperature was already an uncomfortable 80 degrees. The whole building was sweltering and airless, but the elderly woman seemed unaware of the heat. Rosa set her small suitcase down on the worn carpet, pulled a key out of her shiny black handbag, and carefully locked the door, murmuring to herself as she always did these days.

She never stopped talking, although no one could actually make sense of her words. "Excuse me?" the new grocer down the street had said politely just last Tuesday, as Rosa placed twenty kroner on the counter and picked up a liter of milk. But Rosa was immune to such inquiries; she ignored all questions and interruptions. She was constantly in the midst of some important soliloquy and refused to be deterred from finishing her speech.

The other shopkeepers were used to her muttered barrage of

words and had stopped offering their normal pleasantries long ago. Rosa would pack up her groceries in a gray mesh bag and exit the store, leaving a scattering of incomprehensible sentences in her wake.

There was a certain fervent compulsion to her whispering, as if her brain refused to hold back the words any longer, as if they were seeping out through the cracks. As if the container had been somehow damaged; it was no longer water- or air-tight, and the fissures had begun leaking their testimony.

Rosa was starting to feel scared.

She knew she was speaking of things that she had sworn never to reveal, but there was nothing she could do to silence her own words. She tried to whisper them as softly as she could. She spoke as fast as she could. She hoped no one would pay her any mind. She scurried through her errands; she refused to look the shopkeepers in the eye as she made her purchases. Then she would retreat to her small apartment on Frederiksberg Allé, the words spilling out of her nonstop. They hovered in the air, making a little cloud of condensation around her mouth, like puffs of expelled breath on a cold winter day. It took her twenty-four hours to tell the story from beginning to end, and then she would start over, as systematically and precisely as a clock. Never winding down, never missing a word, the same story uncontrollably whispered again and again.

She still managed to go about her daily routines, which had become so ingrained that her body could easily perform all the tasks of washing, cooking, eating, and cleaning without the full cooperation of her mind. But lately the undercurrent of words had been growing perceptibly louder, and in lucid moments Rosa understood that her memory was replaying scenes from her past as persistently as a tape loop. Scenes she had tried so hard to forget. When she still had the full command of her will, she had been able to conceal the words that might prove dangerous. But now her mind had begun to collapse, and what seemed like gibberish to most listeners had the sound of terror to Rosa.

Three weeks ago, in what she perceived as a moment of clarity, Rosa suddenly realized what she would have to do. There were only two people left who shared the secret of her endlessly repeated story. She decided she would have to go see them. She thought that if she looked into their eyes again, the words might finally cease. Then she could spend the rest of her days in blissful silence. She would get on a plane and fly across the ocean. She would look into those faces from her past and renew the vow of silence they had once promised each other. Then maybe the words would stop tumbling out of her mouth. And the memories that she had spent over fifty years trying to suppress would let her go at last.

So on that hot July morning Rosa put the key back in her handbag, picked up her suitcase, and plodded slowly down the four flights of stairs, muttering softly to herself. Her body canted slightly to the right, her gait made awkward by the bag she was carrying. She got into the cab waiting for her in front of the apartment building.

"Kastrup Airport," she said loudly, as if raising her voice was the only way to slice through her whispered monologue. Then she leaned back against the warm leather seat of the Mercedes and closed her eyes.

The driver could feel the old woman's words brushing the back of his neck. His skin prickled, the tiny hairs stood on end. He glanced in the rearview mirror as he pulled the cab away from the curb and slipped into the rush-hour traffic. The old woman with the crimped gray hair and the haggard face looked harmless enough, but he had an eerie feeling about her, and he didn't like it. This was worse than picking up a drunk and worrying about whether the guy was going to throw up all over the back seat. This was much worse. There was something very wrong with this woman.

He was suddenly reminded of a science show he had once watched on TV about sleep patterns, and he thought about the cat that had been turned into a freak by the removal of a small segment of its brain. Sound asleep, the cat would get up and spin in a tight circle, acting out its dreams instead of merely twitching the way a normal cat would. The cat's brain had been short-circuited, the natural restraints had been removed, and the animal had to react physically to the images appearing in its mind.

For some reason this old woman made him think about that cat. There was something odd about her, something off kilter. And the cabbie drove faster than usual, for the first time regretting that there was no quick route through the city to the airport. He didn't even care about the 200-kroner fare; he was just eager to deliver this passenger as swiftly as possible. He wanted her out of his cab.

Twenty-five minutes later, Rosa walked through the entrance of the International Terminal into the smoky haze of the departure hall. Crowds of skimpily clad vacationers heading for the Canary Islands or Mallorca or the Costa del Sol were lined up in front of the check-in counters, chattering animatedly and puffing on their umpteenth cigarettes of the morning. Rosa ignored them all.

She headed straight for the empty Business Class counter and plopped down her ticket and passport.

The young woman in the airline uniform glanced at the documents and said, "I'm sorry, ma'am, but this isn't a Business Class ticket. You'll have to get in line over there." And she pointed to a large group of people waiting to check in under a sign marked "Charters."

But Rosa didn't budge. She gave the counter a sharp rap with the knuckles of her right hand. "*See*-attle," she said loudly, mistakenly putting the stress on the first syllable, as many Scandinavians did. "I'm going to Seattle."

2

Ask Mr. Hansson again whether he's coming over here to work," snapped the Immigration inspector, impatiently drumming his fingers on the counter. He'd been on the job since five a.m., and he was more than ready for lunch, but there were still three other passengers to interrogate after this one.

Margit turned to the tall young man standing next to her and asked him in Swedish, "Are you intending to work while you're in the U.S.?"

"No," said Pär Hansson, shaking his head emphatically, although the sweat was beginning to trickle down his face. "Of course not. I'm here on vacation. I'm just going to visit my cousin."

Margit translated his reply for the inspector, who gave her an exasperated look, as if *she* were the one under scrutiny.

"OK, tell him to put his bags up here," he said wearily. "I want to take a look inside."

As the inspector flipped open the young man's suitcase and

began rummaging around among the carefully packed clothes, Margit sat down on one of the molded plastic chairs lined up in front of the counter. She was sitting in the back of the passport control area of Seattle-Tacoma International Airport. By now she was familiar with the processing routines, and she knew that this case could take some time, especially with Inspector Tyler in charge.

In spite of his air of bored indifference, Tyler had a reputation for diligence and tenacity. His colleagues called him "The Bloodhound," but Margit wondered whether this had more to do with his morose eyes and the sagging folds of his face than with the persistent way in which he carried out his job. At any rate, she was aware that Tyler never liked to give up once his suspicions had been aroused. He had a keen ear for the slight hesitation that might signal a lie (even if he didn't understand the passenger's language). And he was an expert at appraising a person's posture and stance for any sign of nervousness.

Every day hundreds of newly arrived visitors and returning U.S. citizens passed through the rows of glass Immigration booths without incident. Counterfeit documents were a rarity, although Margit had actually been present one day when an inspector spotted a doctored passport and the Ukrainian national was eventually hustled off to jail. And the chance of someone turning up on the undesirable list in the Immigration computers was about equal to winning the state lottery. But those who were suspected of entering the U.S. for purposes other than tourism, or for reasons other than those clearly stated on their visas, were sent off to the back counter for more intensive questioning.

This lanky twenty-something Swede named Pär Hansson was one of the unlucky ones.

Margit couldn't see what had sparked the inspector's initial interest in him, but it was not her job to dig up the truth. She was simply there to translate.

She shook back her shoulder-length blonde hair and gave a little sigh. The air was not the best in this underground, secured section of the airport's South Satellite. And the artificial light and lack of any windows always made Margit feel slightly claustrophobic.

The passport control area consisted of a long hall with the so-called "secondary" counter, where Inspector Tyler presided, at one end. At the opposite end, two steep escalators delivered passengers from the corridors above, which led up to the jetways where all aircraft originating outside the United States were required to park. A series of inspection booths ran the full length of the Immigration hall. In front of the booths a complicated maze of waist-high dividers controlled the flow of arriving passengers, funneling them into snakelike formation. This was the only way to ensure some sense of order when two or three widebody jets arrived in rapid succession, spilling six or seven hundred weary travelers into the limited space. A glassed-in public viewing area some distance away allowed waiting friends and family members to wave mutely to passengers, who then had to proceed downstairs to Customs.

"How's it going?" said a voice on Margit's right, interrupting her daydreaming.

She turned her head to see Brian Blamanis plunk himself down in the seat next to her. His dark-blue Star Air uniform with the red tie and gold insignia gave him such a somber and official appearance. A far cry from the scruffy t-shirts and tattered jeans he had worn when Margit first met him in grad school more than fifteen years ago.

"Hi," she said, giving him a bright smile. "It's going OK, I guess, but I think I might be here for a while."

"What's his story?" asked Brian, gesturing toward the Swedish passenger, who was looking more and more anxious. His shoulders were hunched, his face was flushed, and he began shifting his feet uneasily as Inspector Tyler finished examining the contents of his suitcase and opened up his carry-on bag.

"He's a baker's apprentice from Linköping. He claims he's here to visit his cousin who lives on Mercer Island, but they think he's coming over to work. He speaks some English, but the minute he started getting nervous his language skills fell apart. Do you need me for something else?"

"No, that's OK," said Brian. "I'll call you if I do. The next flight will be here any minute." And then his radio began to squawk and he rushed off to look for a missing guitar for a passenger waiting downstairs in the Customs area.

Margit stretched out her legs, glad that she had chosen linen slacks, a cotton blouse, and a lightweight blazer today. Comfortably casual, but still neat and professional-looking. Ever since she had given up her corporate job with an international import company, she just couldn't stand the thought of putting on a dress and pantyhose in the summer. And the airport was always hot and stuffy, in spite of the air conditioning. Brian was the only reason she was there at all—she didn't usually like to take interpreting jobs.

She had been a freelance translator for years, but she preferred working on technical documents in the privacy of her home office instead of having to interpret on the spot. And she wasn't keen on getting mixed up in the personal stories of the "subjects," as they were called in the interpreting business. People who needed an interpreter were often in trouble of some kind;

they might be tangled up in a legal case or involved in a medical crisis. It was sometimes hard for the interpreter to maintain the necessary distance and objectivity, and Margit had recently been involved in a case that had led to highly unexpected consequences. She definitely preferred working at home.

But a month ago Brian had called and asked whether she would consider coming out to the airport once a week to help with the two charter flights arriving from Stockholm and Copenhagen every Thursday morning during the summer. It was the one day that Scandinavian Airlines didn't operate into Seattle, and Star Air had been contracted as the handling agent for the charters. The company hadn't anticipated any language problems because it was assumed that most Scandinavians spoke English. But the first few weeks had proved more problematic than expected, since the cheap flights were attracting many passengers who had never traveled overseas before. No one on staff spoke any of the Scandinavian languages, and the airport interpreter program, which was run by the Visitors' Bureau, couldn't afford to pay for an extra person. So Star Air decided to hire its own interpreter, and Brian had immediately thought of Margit Andersson.

They had met years ago at an Ibsen seminar at the University of Minnesota and had actually gone out together a few times. But they ended up being friends instead of lovers—a turn of events which they both blamed not on any lack of physical attraction but on the Ingmar Bergman film they had seen on their first date. The chilling scenes from *Cries and Whispers* were enough to quash any budding romance.

Margit smiled wryly as she thought back on the intense literary discussions they had carried on in the cluttered kitchen of Brian's run-down old house, which he shared with five other students. At that time Margit was working on her Masters degree in Scandinavian Studies, while Brian was finishing up his doctoral dissertation on trends in pre-Soviet Baltic fiction. There was a certain poignancy to those university days when nothing mattered but literature, art—and, of course, sex. Before the worries of AIDS, earning a living, and other more mundane adult problems had taken hold.

"Could you have a look at this letter?" Inspector Tyler's voice cut through Margit's reminiscing.

"Oh, sure," she said, getting up and going over to the counter. She scanned the handwritten Swedish words on the sheet of paper and realized that Pär Hansson didn't have a chance.

"Anything relevant?" asked the inspector.

"Well, it's a letter addressed to Mr. Hansson from the Three Crown Bakery in Issaquah. It says: 'We look forward to meeting you on the Monday following your arrival in Seattle. As agreed, we can offer you a temporary position until October 1st, while one of our bakers is on leave of absence. We can't promise you work beyond that date, but things may change by then, and we can always reevaluate the situation when the time comes. Please call us when you arrive to confirm the appointment on Monday morning. And give our greetings to your cousin Ulf.'"

Margit looked up and added, "It's signed by a Göran Hultén."

Inspector Tyler's eyes glittered behind his black-rimmed glasses. He gave a little smirk, unable to hide his satisfaction that once again his instincts had proved right—although this time the victory seemed almost too easy.

"OK, that's it. Tell him to pack up his stuff. He'll be going back home on the next flight. And could you get hold of the airline and tell them that they've got a return passenger?"

Margit hardly needed to translate the inspector's verdict, since the sight of the incriminating letter had immediately crushed the young Swede's last hopes. When he left Stockholm twelve hours earlier, it had never occurred to Pär Hansson that he might be denied entry. He knew it was illegal to work without a permit, but he considered this a minor formality that could be dealt with once he was in the States. And he had expected the U.S. arrival procedures to be as quick and easy as they were in Europe.

In a fog of disbelief he listened to Margit's translated explanation that in less than two hours he would be headed back to Sweden. She told him that the inspector said he had the option to contest the decision and refuse to go. But if he lost the appeal, he would not be allowed to return to the U.S. for at least two years. If he went home now, he could apply for the appropriate work permit, and there would be no prohibition against his return. With a groan Pär Hansson sank down onto a chair and put his head in his hands.

At that moment a loud commotion erupted at the other end of the hall, and Margit turned around to see what was going on.

The second charter flight of the morning had obviously just arrived because a new swarm of passengers was coming down the escalators and had begun to file into the maze in front of the Immigration booths. But something was happening on the escalator to the right, which was close to the glassed-in public viewing area. Halfway down the slowly descending stairs, an old woman in a blue dress was madly waving her arms around and giving one long shriek after another. People were scrambling to get out of her way, dashing down the remaining steps as fast as they could go. Those standing behind her had turned around in alarm, attempting to retreat backwards, but they were penned in by the crowd still pouring onto the escalator from above.

Margit took one look at the chaotic scene and set off running. She reached the escalator just as the old woman came to the bottom.

Clearly oblivious to anything but her own panic, the woman failed to step off in time, and she abruptly pitched forward as her feet hit the edge of the metal landing. Margit bent over the woman's collapsed form, lifted her under the arms, and dragged her away from the onslaught of passengers continuing to come down the escalator. Then she laid her down gently on the carpet and knelt beside her, ignoring the other people milling around.

The old woman's face had lost all color, her eyes were closed tight, and her breath was coming in short little gasps. She had a small cut on her forehead, and a rivulet of blood was seeping down past her right ear and into the collar of her blue dress. She had stopped screaming when she fell, but now her lips began to move, as if she wanted to say something.

Margit bent closer, patted her on the shoulder, and murmured in English, "It's OK, take it easy."

Suddenly the woman's eyes flew open, and she looked up at Margit with an expression of bewilderment that instantly gave way to fear. She uttered two carefully enunciated words and then looked as if she might start shrieking again. Instead, her eyes fell shut, her face went slack, and her head rolled limply to the side.

In shock, Margit was barely aware of someone gripping her by the elbow and pulling her to her feet.

"The medics are here now," she heard Brian say, sounding as if he were talking underwater. "Come on, let's go. There's nothing more we can do."

3

Half an hour later, Margit was still feeling shaky as she sat in the fluorescent glare of the deserted Immigration office. The inspectors were all busy processing passengers on a flight from Tokyo that had just arrived, more than three hours late. Margit sipped lukewarm water from a paper cup, noting that her hand was trembling slightly.

She was normally good in emergencies, able to assess the situation quickly and then take the appropriate action. She had the unconscious ability to separate her own emotions from whatever was happening. When she knelt down beside the old woman and touched her shoulder, Margit had literally taken a step back from herself, as if she were dispassionately observing the scene from a few feet away. It was only afterwards that her semblance of calm would crumble, and her body would display all the normal symptoms of shock and fear.

Margit picked up a copy of *Sports Illustrated* that was lying on the gray metal desk in front of her and riffled through the pages. For a full minute she stared at the enormous image of a boxer's swollen face before she even noticed his bloody right ear.

"My God," she moaned, dropping the magazine to the floor, as she saw in her mind the blood trickling from the old woman's forehead.

"You OK?" asked Brian as he came into the office with a sullen-looking kid in tow. Pinned to the boy's shirt was a red plastic button with the initials "U.M." in bright yellow.

"I think so," said Margit, shrugging her shoulders and smiling weakly. "Who's this?"

"This is Erik. We're waiting for his mom to get here."

Margit could hear the barely disguised tone of disapproval in Brian's voice. Just last week he had complained to her about the plight of too many Unaccompanied Minors—the official term for kids under the age of twelve who were traveling alone. People would entrust their children to an airline, expecting strangers to shepherd them safely to their destination. But then some parents would actually fail to show up at the airport on time to pick up their kids. Brian had told Margit that on a few occasions it had even taken until the next day to locate the errant guardian. In those cases the ground staff was forced to assume the responsibility of temporary custody.

Brian had two kids of his own, so all his protective instincts were aroused by such derelict behavior. He said it was bad enough that a lot of these U.M.s were regularly shuttled back and forth between their divorced parents, one on each side of the ocean. But he hated to see their expressions of disappointment harden into stony resignation when no one showed up to meet them.

"Have a seat over there," Brian told the boy kindly, pointing to a scuffed wooden chair near the door. "This will only take a minute."

"So what did the medics say?" asked Margit quietly as Brian perched on the edge of the desk where she was sitting.

"An apparent heart attack," he said. "They did everything they could to revive her, but they couldn't bring her back."

Margit suddenly thought about the first time she had ever seen a dead body. That happened in an airport too—years ago, only a few weeks after she had started her job with H. Weisman Imports. She was waiting to check in for a flight from San Francisco to Seattle when a ticket agent behind the counter abruptly keeled over and fell to the floor without uttering a sound. Margit clearly remembered the peculiar gray pallor of the man's face and the vacant stare of his eyes. The medics arrived in minutes and immediately placed the man on the halted baggage belt, since it was the only available space in those cramped quarters. They worked on him furiously but were unable to save his life. A teenage girl standing in line behind Margit had started to sob uncontrollably as the dead man was lifted onto a gurney and wheeled briskly away through the back offices.

Margit blinked rapidly, as if to erase from her memory the ignominy of that poor man dying on a conveyor belt surrounded by baggage. The second time she had seen a dead body was only a few months ago, but she was not going to think about that. She tucked a strand of hair behind her ear and looked up at Brian.

"Did you find out who she was?"

"Her name was Rosa Nørgaard. A Danish woman from Copenhagen. She had a round-trip ticket, and she was due to fly back next week. We couldn't find anyone waiting to meet her, and she didn't seem to have any kind of address book in her purse. That's all we really know about her so far. The airport police are handling the matter."

Brian turned down the rapid-fire chatter issuing from his radio. His colleagues were busy upstairs at the gate with preparations for the departing flight.

"By the way, the police said they'll need to get a statement from you. Officer Reston is downstairs in Customs and wants to talk to you as soon as it's convenient. Are you feeling up to it right now? We're pretty much done here for today, anyway. I just have to pick up the Swedish guy and put him on the return flight."

"OK," said Margit. "I'll stop by to see you at the Star Air counter before I go home."

Brian nodded, slipped off the desk, and motioned to the boy to follow him. Then they both rushed out of the room.

Margit stood up slowly, smoothing out the wrinkles in her linen slacks. She took her jade-green blazer from the back of the chair and put it on. A glance at her watch told her that it was almost one o'clock.

She wondered why Brian thought the old woman was a Dane. Her last name sounded Danish enough, although Brian might have mispronounced it. He was fluent in Latvian, Estonian, and Russian, but his knowledge of the Nordic languages was limited to a few polite phrases.

As Margit left the Immigration office, making sure that the door locked securely behind her, she thought about the two words the old woman had uttered before she died. Those words were definitely Swedish, not Danish.

"*Inte honom!*" Rosa Nørgaard had said quite clearly, with that unmistakable look of terror in her eyes. "Not him!"

27

4

Margit walked past the secondary counter, heading for the escalator that would take her downstairs to Customs. She noticed that Tyler was still on the job, speaking through a Japanese interpreter to a man wearing a rumpled gray suit. The inspector was looking downright surly by now, having missed a chance to grab any lunch before the Tokyo flight arrived.

Give that man some food, thought Margit sympathetically. She was all too familiar with the insidious effects of low blood sugar. She had taken to carrying peppermint Lifesavers in her pocket and an apple or a couple of crackers in her bag—anything to curb the awful feeling of cranky edginess that would come over her if she let too much time pass in between meals.

At the top of the escalator, Margit paused for a moment to survey the scene below.

Several hundred passengers were crowded around an enormous, oval-shaped baggage belt, jostling each other for front-row positions as they waited impatiently for their suitcases to arrive. Suddenly an orange light began to flash and the belt started moving. A bright green sports bag emerged from the depths of the center chute, teetered on the rim for a second, and then tumbled onto the revolving belt, followed by a steady stream of suitcases in all shapes and sizes.

Frenzy reigned. People leaped forward, shouting, "There it is!" or the equivalent in a multitude of languages, shoving other passengers aside in their haste to pull the bags off the belt. Customs officers sprang into action, some of them circulating among the crowd, others manning the inspection stations.

Margit gave a nod of recognition as she descended into the noisy tumult of the Customs area. She had been through here so many times before, coming home from a visit to her Scandinavian relatives or returning from yet another business trip to Europe. Just a few months ago she had stood at that very baggage belt in the company of a rather attractive Seattle police detective. He had been her constant companion during a memorable week in Copenhagen. Margit felt again a pang of regret that she hadn't returned his call after he left a message on her answering machine a few days later. But Joe was in town at the time, and she was feeling confused, to say the least. The detective hadn't called again.

As Margit made her way toward the inspection stations, her attention was caught by a little beagle trotting past. He was pulling on his leash as he moved from suitcase to suitcase, sniffing vigorously.

"Oh, what a cute dog," said a woman, bending down with her hand stretched out.

"Please don't pet him, ma'am," said the officer holding the dog's leash. "He has a job to do. He's looking for any meat or plants that people might have brought with them." And he pointed to the cloth sign draped over the beagle's back which said: "Your U.S. Department of Agriculture at Work."

Suddenly a baggage cart rammed hard into the back of Margit's leg, and she felt a rush of fury. She whirled around, ready to spit out an angry rebuke. But the perpetrator was a tiny three-year-old with impish eyes, who gurgled happily as he looked up at the tall blonde woman blocking the path of his cart.

Margit smiled and stepped aside, realizing that she was over-reacting. Her nerves were still frazzled from witnessing the old woman's death.

"Calm down," she told herself, taking two deep breaths before she continued to weave her way through the crowd to the far side of the Customs area. She had spotted Gary Hernandez, one of the officers she had done quite a bit of interpreting for during the past month. He was an ex-military man with a brusque manner and stern face, but he turned out to have a good sense of humor. And he was always giving Margit useful advice about working in the arrivals area.

"Don't ever rub your eyes or touch your face," he had told her one day, for example. "Wash your hands thoroughly when you're done in here. You never know what kind of germs you might have picked up. We get exposed to all sorts of stuff."

As Margit approached the row of inspection stations, Officer Hernandez glanced up and waved her over with a look of relief. He was a stocky man with graying, buzz-cut hair. A gold chain was visible in the open neck of his regulation shirt with the Customs insignia on the sleeves.

"Hey, Margit," he shouted, "do you know any French?"

"A little," she said, glancing at the passenger in the Tour de France t-shirt that he was apparently trying to communicate with. A large leather suitcase stood on the low inspection counter between them.

"The Ag dog got all excited about this guy's bag. Ask him what's inside."

Margit paused for a moment, reaching into her mind for remnants of the French that she had learned in college, buried under all the layers of other languages she used more frequently.

"*Monsieur, qu'est-ce que vous avez dans votre valise?*"

"*Des oiseaux*," said the Frenchman, beaming happily.

"*Comment?*"

"*Des oiseaux*," he repeated.

Margit turned to the Customs officer and said uncertainly, "Well, he claims he has birds in his suitcase."

"Birds?" Hernandez stared at her for a moment, and then grinned. "OK, let's have a look."

The Frenchman obligingly opened up his suitcase and there in the midst of his clothing, wrapped carefully in plastic, were three bloody birds, with their heads and feet cut off.

Margit stared at the mutilated corpses and felt suddenly sick. This is too much, she thought with a shudder. Way too much for one day.

It turned out that the man was a hunter, bringing with him the main course for a family feast. And he had done his homework well. A quick consultation with the Agriculture supervisor revealed that it was legal to import that type of bird as long as the head and feet had been removed, since that was the only way to avoid the transmission of any disease.

"Never know what we're going to find," said Hernandez, shaking his head as the Frenchman picked up his suitcase and set off for the exit.

"Thanks for your help," he added, turning to Margit. "Done for the day now?"

"Uh-huh," she murmured, still feeling a little queasy from

the sight of those birds. Then she remembered why she had come down to Customs in the first place. "Well, actually, I'm supposed to talk to an Officer Reston. Have you seen him?"

"Her, not him," said Hernandez, glancing up from the Declaration form he was stamping. "That's her over there." And he pointed to a woman wearing the black uniform of the airport police. She was standing alone at the next station, bending over a suitcase which lay open next to a patent leather handbag.

"Thanks," said Margit and walked over to the long, low counter. Clothing and other personal articles were neatly stacked along its surface.

"Officer Reston? I'm Margit Andersson. I heard that you wanted to see me."

"Oh, yes. You're the interpreter. Great." The officer straightened up and gave Margit a friendly nod. She was of Asian extraction, with delicate features and intense brown eyes. Her hair was cut in a blunt pageboy style. "I just need to ask you a few questions. Have a seat and I'll be with you in a minute."

Margit looked around for a chair but finding none, sat down on the edge of the counter. This brought her to eye level with the petite officer, who was frowning slightly as she carefully examined each item from the suitcase and then efficiently put everything back in place. A paperback book ended up on top. Margit turned her head sideways to look at the cover. It was a volume of poetry by Tove Ditlevsen, one of her favorite Danish authors.

She bent closer and looked at the tag attached to the suitcase handle. "Rosa Nørgaard," it said in spidery handwriting, followed by an address in Frederiksberg. Margit knew that part of Copenhagen well—a district on the western edge of the city that was a mixture of elegant but drafty old villas and enormous blocks of apartment buildings dating from the turn of the century.

"So she does have a Danish name, after all," said Margit.

"Why does that surprise you?" asked Reston, as she closed up the old woman's suitcase and began emptying out the contents of the handbag.

"Because the last words I heard her speak were Swedish, not Danish. She said 'Not him!' and the words were definitely Swedish."

"'Not him'?" repeated the officer, pausing in her work. "That's an odd thing to say. Was that all? She didn't say anything else?"

"No, but she was terrified. I could see it in her eyes."

Reston gave Margit a long, appraising look, and then nodded. She picked up a clipboard, moved over to the podium at the end of the counter, and began writing rapidly.

Margit noticed Rosa Nørgaard's passport lying on the counter. All the countries belonging to the European Union now issued the same beet-colored passport, but each country had its own name stamped in gold on the front. This one said "DANMARK." She picked it up and opened it with curiosity.

"Rosa Nørgaard, née Lindqvist," she read. "Date of birth: 22 December 1926. Place of birth: Hälsingborg, Sweden."

So that's it, thought Margit. She must have been a naturalized Dane, but Swedish was her first language, and in a moment of crisis she reverted to her mother tongue. It was funny how languages were so deeply embedded in a person's psyche.

Margit thought about her own father who was born in Uppsala but who had lived in St. Paul for forty-five years now. He spoke perfectly fluent English with only a trace of an accent. But whenever he was feeling excited or stressed, Swedish words would occasionally pop up in the middle of his sentences. And to this day, Margit's mother counted out her knitting stitches in

Danish, not English. Her native language would always come more naturally to her.

"Do you know what this is?"

Margit gave a start and looked up. Officer Reston was holding out her hand with a small silver pendant nestled in the palm.

"It's a Thor's hammer," said Margit, recognizing the familiar anchorlike shape at once. "It's a popular kind of jewelry in Scandinavia. I have a necklace like that myself."

"Thor—wasn't he the Nordic god of war?"

"No," said Margit, shaking her head. "Thor was a great warrior, but he used his powers to fend off the demons of destruction. The hammer was a symbol of his strength, and in pagan times people wore it as a protective talisman."

The police officer raised her eyebrows at Margit's earnest reply, which prompted her to add, "I was a big mythology fan when I was a kid."

Reston nodded and let the necklace slip onto the counter. Margit noticed that the chain was broken.

"Did you find it in her purse?" she asked.

"No, we found it in her hand," said the officer, picking up the clipboard again and scribbling a note. "She was clutching it in her hand when she died."

5

W hat a day," said Brian as he escorted Margit into the Star Air office behind the ticket counter in the main terminal. "Must be the worst one of the summer so far. Eight wheelchair passengers, five U.M.s, and one denied entry—not to mention the woman who had a heart attack. Then we had catering problems that delayed the second outbound flight until a few minutes ago. Plus we found out that a whole container of baggage is still sitting on the tarmac in Copenhagen. I've got two agents stuck in Customs filling out baggage claim forms for some very unhappy passengers."

Brian had recently been promoted to assistant station manager, but Margit wasn't sure the extra pay was worth it. The responsibility of overseeing the "front line," as the ground staff was called in the airline industry, was already having a noticeable effect on her friend. He seemed unusually nervous and tense, and his brown hair had more gray in it than Margit remembered. She was worried about him, and she promised herself to have a talk with his wife Cynthia, who was in her book club.

Margit sat down at the big round table in the corner where the staff usually relaxed in between flights. Brian put his radio into the stand on the shelf to recharge the battery and then took off his jacket before he sat down beside her. Sharon and Thomas were the only other agents in the office at the moment. They were busy entering flight information in the computer and getting things ready for the next charter, due in at three o'clock from Frankfurt. Everyone else was either at the ticket counter or out at the departure gates. Star Air operated several domestic flights of its own each day, but they were a breeze to handle compared to the headaches of coping with international charters.

"Did the kid's mother ever show up?" asked Margit. Brian nodded as he picked up a sandwich from a tray on the table and began wolfing it down.

"Yeah, the woman finally showed up—two hours late. Said she was out shopping and lost track of the time. Can you believe it?" He scooted the tray of sandwiches over toward Margit. "Help yourself."

"No thanks," she said, since they all seemed to contain some kind of meat. She was surprised that Brian didn't remember she was a vegetarian. Good thing she'd grabbed a slice of cheese pizza on her way back from the South Satellite. Not the best choice for someone who was trying to lose a few pounds, but she'd been too rushed in the morning to fix a bag lunch. Her cat Gregor had stayed out all night, and it took her almost half an hour to track him down, curled up asleep under the neighbor's back porch.

"By the way, did the police say anything else about Mrs. Nørgaard?" Brian asked.

"Not really," said Margit. "They still don't know why she was coming over here, and they didn't find a clue to any American friends or relatives when they went through her luggage.

Officer Reston said they were going to contact the Danish police about her. She hadn't been officially admitted to the U.S. before she died, so I guess there are legal complications. I didn't understand it all. But apparently there's going to be an autopsy to determine the cause of death, even though it seemed clear that she died of a heart attack."

Margit frowned. "Do you think it's possible for somebody to die of fright?"

Brian gave her a surprised look and said, "I don't know."

Then he turned his head to the left as static began to spew out of the cut channel, a special radio that linked the office to the cockpits of arriving and departing Star Air flights whenever they were within range of the airport.

He got up and went over to adjust a dial. The crackling noise slipped into a high-pitched screech, and then a voice suddenly boomed out, "So who's ahead?"

Brian laughed and turned to his colleagues. "Anybody know the score?"

"The Yankees are leading, five to three," said Sharon, looking up from her computer screen.

Brian picked up the microphone and pressed in the "talk" button. "Your team's winning, Captain. Five to three."

"Great. See you next week."

"Have a good flight."

Brian took two bottles of lime-flavored Talking Rain out of the small fridge against the wall and handed one to Margit before he sat down again. "A Norwegian pilot, but he's nuts about baseball."

Sports and sex seemed to be the main topics of conversation among the airline staff, especially if the station manager, Don Schmidt, was present. He was a walking encyclopedia of baseball and football statistics, and his language was peppered with sports terms. He regarded himself as the Star Air "coach," and the staff was his "team"—but not all players were equal.

From her first day on the job, Margit had noted a certain homophobic slant to Schmidt's humor, which she found especially offensive. And his clumsy attempts to flirt with her had also quickly reached the annoying stage. But since she was only working for him on a temporary basis, she decided that cold civility was the proper course of action—although she did have to put her foot down when he started referring to her as the "interpreter girl." She told Schmidt quite firmly that at the age of forty she was no longer a girl.

Aside from that, she had decided that any further confrontation would be pointless with a man who proudly referred to himself as the "Stuttgart Stud." Margit seriously doubted there was any truth to this self-aggrandizing nickname; she strongly suspected that he was all talk and no action. But Brian told her there had been rumblings among the female employees about pressing charges for sexual harassment. So far, nothing had come of it. Margit did her best to stay out of Schmidt's way, and she steadfastly refused to laugh at his reactionary jokes.

"I'm worn out," she told Brian, propping her chin on her hand. "How can you stand the pace? I only come out here once a week, and already I'm starting to feel an aversion to crowds."

"Guess I'm just used to it by now," he said with a weary smile, running his hand through his hair. "After eight years in this business, a certain amount of chaos seems normal."

"Done any translating lately?" Margit asked. She knew this was a sore point, but sometimes it was the duty of old friends to bring up uncomfortable topics. Especially if there were issues still unresolved.

"Nope," said Brian, evading her glance. And then he changed

the subject and started rambling on about his daughter's new boyfriend.

Brian Blamanis had once been considered the most promising of a generation of young American translators working with Russian and Baltic fiction. His translations of two classic Latvian novels were hailed as particularly brilliant. And his work with the plays of an experimental Russian writer had won him a prestigious prize. By the mid-eighties Brian had half a dozen highly acclaimed, published translations to his name. At the time, he was teaching at a small Midwest college, giving seminars on the art of translation and the importance of literature in twentieth-century life. His passion for his subject became legendary among his students, but Brian soon realized that teaching was diverting his energies from his real work. Finally, he quit his job to devote himself full-time to literary translation.

Back then, his wife Cynthia was still earning the lion's share of their income with her accounting business, but Brian had high hopes that one day he could support his family through his book translations.

Margit had followed his achievements with interest, as she gave up her own academic career and took a job in the corporate world.

Then in 1986, Brian was commissioned to translate a literary thriller called *Sinister Cinnamon* by an Estonian author completely unknown outside his own country. To the surprise of everyone — including the American publisher — the novel hit it big, landing on all the bestseller lists. But it turned out to be a bitter experience for Brian.

Cynthia later confided to Margit that he had not been able to persuade the publisher to include any kind of royalty clause in his contract. And the per-word fee they offered him was ludicrous, but Brian had ended up accepting the less than favorable terms. He liked the book and didn't want to lose the job to another translator. And he knew that in the eyes of that particular publisher, translators were little more than interchangeable typists. Cost always outweighed reputation. *Sinister Cinnamon* became a smash hit, selling in the millions, and everyone involved with the project raked in the dough—except Brian.

He tried to appeal to the publisher's sense of fairness, since the financial success of the book was largely due to the excellence of his translation. But the company reminded him of the terms of his contract and then told him to "sit back and enjoy the good reviews."

Brian's reply was a one-line quote from the legendary R&B singer, Lazy Lester: "The publicity was great, but you can't eat a publicity sandwich."

Margit once asked him why he didn't hire a lawyer, but Brian told her the cost of litigation would have been astronomical, and he simply couldn't afford it.

After that fiasco he seemed to lose all heart for literary translation work, even though he learned that his was not an isolated case. He heard from other, much more famous translators that they had also been excluded from sharing in the profits of their work, and several cases involved the same publisher. But with two young children to support, Brian needed a steady income, and he didn't want to go back to teaching. His wife had relatives in Washington state, so they decided to head for the West Coast. And when the Star Air job in Seattle came up, he was glad to get it. He had been with the company ever since.

Margit took another sip of water and glanced over at Brian, who had stopped talking and was absent-mindedly rolling a bottle cap around on the table. She warned herself not to broach the topic again, but her curiosity got the better of her, and she just had to ask.

"I was watching the Hollywood Minute on CNN last night," she said. "And I saw that they're making a film out of *Sinister Cinnamon*. Did you get any cash from the movie deal?"

"You bet," said Brian, looking at her with a strange glint in his eye. "The publisher paid me $500 for the use of my translation for the script. I hear it's going to be a thirty-million-dollar movie."

"Ouch," said Margit, wishing she hadn't brought it up.

Just then the back door to the office flew open and Don Schmidt charged into the room with five or six of his "team" behind him, all of them laughing and talking loudly. They were returning from the departure gate in the South Satellite, relieved that another flight was finally gone.

Schmidt strode over to the stereo system that was installed above the refrigerator and snapped on the radio. Margit cringed as she recognized the saccharine strains of the tune swelling from the speakers. No one was allowed to change the station, which seemed to have only three songs in its repertoire: "The Impossible Dream," "People," and "I Left My Heart in San Francisco." Today it was Don Quixote's turn.

"OK, team, listen up," shouted Schmidt as he moved over to his favorite command post next to the huge company safe. He leaned against the armored door, smugly aware that all attention was now focused on him. He was the only male staff member not wearing a tie. Instead, his white short-sleeved shirt was open halfway down, revealing a mat of dark hair against his tan chest.

Margit leaned over and whispered to Brian, "In Danish we call that a 'gorilla tie.'"

Brian snorted as the station manager launched into his usual pep talk about getting ready for the next "inning." He had devised his own code—not entirely logical—for the roster of staff positions required to cover each flight. Brian was referred to as the "pitcher," the cashier was the "catcher," and the gate agent was the "outfielder." The ticket counter positions were known as "first," "second," and "third" base. The staff locker area was the "dugout." And Schmidt's private office was, of course, "home plate." Before each flight, he would hand out the work assignments.

Brian had told Margit that in the wintertime, the station manager switched to football terminology. She was glad she wouldn't be around for that.

"Guess I'll be taking off," said Margit after the speech was over and everyone had settled into their afternoon routines.

"Don't work too hard," she added, giving Brian a pat on the back as he got up to retrieve his recharged radio from the stand.

"I won't," he said with a smile. "See you next week."

Margit headed for the door, but as she passed the station manager's office, Schmidt motioned for her to step inside.

"Hey Margit, there was somebody out at the gate who really has the hots for you," he said with a snicker.

"What do you mean?"

"This guy came up and asked me your name and all kinds of questions about you, so I gave him your phone number."

"You *what?*" gasped Margit, outraged.

"Just kidding," said Schmidt. "Don't worry. Besides, the guy was way too old for you. Could have been your father. Had some weird accent too. Definitely not your type." And he went back to reading the sports page.

As if he has any idea what kind of man I'd be interested in, fumed Margit as she stepped out into the dazzling sunshine a few minutes later.

What I need right now is an espresso, she thought as she walked toward the parking garage. A double.

6

There's something so vulgar about orchids," whispered Margit to herself as she peered into a glass display case inside the Conservatory at Volunteer Park. The dense humidity of the greenhouse was making her ponytail cling limply to the back of her neck, and her blouse was sticking unpleasantly to her skin. Why would anyone find orchids beautiful or romantic? To her, they seemed hideous and spiderlike, furtively hiding out in the moist green foliage. As menacing as deadly nightshade, monkshood, henbane, or belladonna—all those poisonous plants she had once read about when she was translating a toxicology manual.

Margit bent closer to examine a deep purple orchid with frilly petals and threads of dark-pink and yellow emanating from the center. What was it that gave these flowers such an alien and ominous look?

She straightened up and decided to head for the relative serenity of the cactus room. At least there the danger was obvious. The spikes and thorns were all out in the open, defying too close an approach.

She wandered through the room bristling with prickly plants. No one else was around.

It was almost five o'clock on Friday evening, and most people were just getting off work, anxious to start their weekend and cursing at the traffic that was getting as bad as in L.A. It had taken Margit an extra twenty minutes to make the drive from her house in West Seattle to Volunteer Park, even though she took the alternative route over Beacon Hill. Another Mariners game at the Kingdome had turned I-5 into a parking lot.

"Just wait until they build the new stadiums," she had complained to her friend Renny on the phone the night before as they made plans to meet at the Conservatory before going to an art opening nearby. "We'll never be able to get into town."

"I know," said Renny. "What a nightmare. Why couldn't they put the damn things out in the 'burbs where there's more space? But speaking of sports, how'd it go at the airport? Is the 'coach' still pestering you?"

"No, I stay out of his way, and I actually think he's a little intimidated by me. Brian says he has a real problem with smart women. But you wouldn't believe what a day I had."

And Margit told Renny about the frightened old woman who had died in the Immigration hall.

Renny was sympathetic, although it was clear that the event had no effect on her impression that the airport must be an exciting place to work.

"All those people coming and going," she had said, dreamily, when Margit first told her about the airport assignment. "All those planes taking off for exotic places on the other side of the world." Renny obviously shared the common misconception that working for an airline was a glamor job.

Margit knew better. Traveling was a stressful business. She

had heard Brian's stories about flight delays that turned dignified lawyers into sniveling five-year-olds, throwing temper tan-
trums right at the ticket counter. People actually expected the
airline staff to be able to predict when the fog would lift or when
a sudden blizzard might be over.

"If the passengers get really belligerent," Brian had told her,
"I just look them in the eye and say 'I'm sorry, but it's an act of
God.' That usually shuts them up."

Margit knew that it was not uncommon for the ground staff
to work sixteen-hour shifts, especially when bad weather wreaked
havoc with the airline schedules. She knew about the pressures
of getting aircraft serviced and turned around on time, because
every extra minute spent on the ground meant lost revenues for
the company. And she had seen some of the wacky people who
regularly turned up at the airport, keeping the staff constantly
on the alert for security problems.

As for the travel benefits that were so envied by the general
public, it turned out that they weren't such a deal after all. Brian
had explained that airline employees were eligible for tickets dis-
counted as much as 90%, but they had to travel on a standby
basis, which could be unbelievably nerve-wracking. If there were
any leftover seats on a flight, they were assigned to anxiously
waiting employees, according to a rigorously enforced hierar-
chy, just before departure time. In high season and on the more
popular routes, standby seats were especially hard to come by. It
had once taken Brian and Cynthia an exhausting forty-five hours
and seven different flights to make it back from Athens.

"Sometimes," Brian had said, "it's just a lot easier to stay
home."

Margit shook her head as she wandered down an aisle in
the cactus room, glad that her airport interpreting job was only

temporary. It was just too hectic for her taste. She wondered whether Brian felt any sense of accomplishment at the end of a work week—after all, it was no small task to get hundreds of people safely on their way. She knew that some airline employees actually thrived on the daily pressure, finding the mad frenzy stimulating and fun. But Margit doubted that Brian still shared those feelings after eight numbing years on the job.

She touched the Thor's hammer she was wearing on a silver chain. On impulse she had taken the necklace out of her jewelry box that morning and decided to wear it. A small gesture of respect for the woman who had died.

Or maybe Margit was feeling as if she could use some of Thor's protective powers herself. She was often plagued by nightmares, but at three in the morning she was jolted awake by a dream she hadn't had in years—she was once again riding through the desolate wartime scene that had haunted so many of her childhood nights.

Now Margit breathed in the hot dry air of the greenhouse, wondering what had happened to Renny—she wasn't usually late. The dull greens and soft grays of the spiny cactuses were actually a soothing sight, making Margit almost forget about the obtuse business documents she had spent all day translating from Swedish. It was another rush job from the Koivisto Translation Agency in Belltown, her main client these days. But at least she had been able to work at home.

The arid setting of the cactus room inevitably reminded Margit of New Mexico, and she couldn't help thinking about her last visit to the Southwest to see Joe.

That was back in April, not long after her return from Copenhagen. They had spent several days together at a charming bed-and-breakfast in Taos, and on the surface everything seemed the same as usual between them. They roamed through dozens of art galleries, they drank coffee in the bookstore café, and they spent languorous hours in bed. The sex was still great, but one morning after a particularly inventive round of contortions, Margit had the sudden suspicion that it was the artist in Joe who took the most pleasure in their lovemaking—as if he were subconsciously posing their bodies for one of his sculptures.

For the rest of the day, she couldn't get this idea out of her mind. In the afternoon they ran into the painter Frank Sanchez on the street, and as he and Joe began talking shop, Margit took a few steps back and gazed at her lover intently.

He was handsome all right, there was no doubt about that. At fifty his face had a lean, rugged look to it, and he had the sparkling eyes that Margit always found so irresistible in a man. His brown hair was curly and tousled, and still as plentiful as a boy's. He was slightly taller than Margit, and disgustingly fit from all the heavy labor involved in constructing his mammoth sculptures. Her own more sedentary type of work had forced Margit to adopt a daily exercise routine, which she sometimes resented.

As Margit watched Joe talking animatedly to his colleague, it dawned on her that she was looking at a man in love. His whole body radiated joy. But he was talking about his latest project—not about her. For the first time she realized that she was jealous of Joe's passion for his art. And it occurred to her that there had always been a small part of Joe that he held back, even in moments of sexual surrender.

"It's not that I think couples should share absolutely everything," Margit later told Renny, hoping that as an artist her friend might have some special insight into the situation. "But I'm starting to think that Joe loves his work so fiercely that he can't give his heart fully to anything or anyone else. Or at least not to me."

After that trip to New Mexico, Margit began to discover more and more things about Joe that annoyed her. She found fault with little personal habits that she had previously thought endearing, and she started snapping at him on the phone.

When Joe called to invite Margit to join him for a weekend in Tucson while he supervised the installation of a new sculpture, she abruptly declined. When she failed to give him an adequate reason for her refusal, Joe finally lost his temper and roared, "What the hell is going on?"

Margit tearfully had to admit that she was having doubts about their relationship. "I need some time to think things over," she told him. "I can't explain it any better than that. I just need some time alone."

Joe was understandably hurt and angry, but he reluctantly agreed to her request. They had had a few more awkward phone conversations, but they hadn't seen each other since.

When Margit got home from the airport the day before and played the messages on her answering machine, she found Bonnie Raitt's voice plaintively singing "Baby Come Back."

Suddenly something thumped Margit on the shoulder.

"My God!" she shrieked, spinning around. Her right hand brushed against the thick ridges of a cactus covered with needle-sharp fuzz. Prickles of pain shot through her fingers.

"Geez, I'm sorry, Margit." Renny was standing there with her hand raised, looking a little startled herself. "Didn't you hear me talking to you? I said, 'Wow, that's a nasty-looking plant, don't go any closer.' And then you nodded your head, so I thought for sure you heard me. I didn't mean to scare you." She gave her friend a contrite smile and patted her on the shoulder again.

"That's OK. I guess I forgot where I was. I was thinking

about Joe." To avoid saying anything more, Margit held her hand up close to her face and began pulling out the tiny white cactus spines embedded in her skin.

"Sorry I'm late," said Renny. "I went to visit my Aunt Olive with my father, and then we got stuck in the baseball traffic."

"How's she doing?" asked Margit.

Renny's aunt had been diagnosed with Alzheimer's, and over the past few months her mind had begun to deteriorate rapidly.

"Not so good," said Renny. "I'm not sure she even recognizes me anymore. Today she was scolding my father about his white fiancée—she seemed to think it was 1946 again. Aunt Olive never could stand my mother."

Renny shook her head, making her gold earrings shimmer against her warm brown skin. She had inherited her father's features and coloring, but she had the green eyes of her German mother. She had been given her mother's name too: Renate, although she had never been called anything but Renny.

"Want to look at the other wing of the Conservatory?"

"No," said Margit. "I think I've seen enough. Let's go."

They headed toward the main entrance, past the orchid cases, the giant banana trees, and some other tropical plants with enormous fanlike leaves.

"Just like the fishermen use in Sulawesi," said Renny, putting out her hand to stroke the glossy green lobes. "I saw a show on the Discovery Channel about it. The fisherman attaches a huge leaf like this one to his fishing line, sort of like a kite, to keep the bait hovering just below the surface of the water. Then he lies back in his boat with his eyes on the sky and lazily waits for the kite to bob up and down—which tells him that a garfish has swallowed his spiderweb bait. Amazing technique, huh?"

"Incredible," said Margit, but she wasn't really paying attention.

They walked out the front door, glad to be met by a cool breeze. A welcome change after the cloying heat of the greenhouse.

"Where's this art opening we're going to?" asked Margit, thinking about the last show Renny had taken her to. The cavernous studio had been filled with towering phallic sculptures that surprised even Renny. "Wow," she had exclaimed, "I feel so fertile in here."

Margit hoped today's show would be a little tamer. She was in no mood for blatant sexual symbolism.

"It's over on Prospect," said Renny. "In one of those huge mansions. Let's leave your car here and walk."

She put on her sunglasses and slung the strap of her red leather bag over her shoulder. As a painter, Renny loved strong colors. Today she was wearing an orange tank top that accentuated her firm breasts and sinewy arms. The soft fabric of her blue and white skirt swirled around her bare legs, and her white sandals slapped faintly against the pavement.

"What's with all the elderly Scandinavians in this town?" she said suddenly, turning her head to look at Margit as they walked through the park. "They seem to be dropping like flies lately."

"What do you mean?"

"First the woman at the airport, and now the one on Queen Anne. Didn't you see the newspaper?"

"You know I never read the paper. Watching the national news on TV is bad enough, but all those sleazy local crimes just make me depressed."

"Maybe I shouldn't tell you about this one either," teased Renny.

"Come on. Tell me what it is."

"Well, the article caught my eye because I've been reading a great historical mystery that's set in sixteenth-century Prague, and I stumbled on the word 'defenestration' and had to look it up. Do you know what it means?"

"As a matter of fact, I do," said Margit, suddenly recalling a scene from the movie *Braveheart*. "It means the act of throwing someone out the window, usually to their death."

"That's right. Anyway, the headline in the paper said 'Retired Doctor Pushed From Window.' Her name was Gudrun Madsen, and she was apparently in her late seventies. A pediatrician who emigrated to the U.S. from Denmark a long time ago. Her body was found lying on the ground under the window of her fifth-floor condominium around midnight. The police thought it might be a suicide until they got into the woman's apartment and found signs of a struggle. By the way, they quoted your friend Detective Tristano in the paper—he must be in charge of the case."

Margit was surprised to find herself blushing.

"Hey, you know what?" said Renny, stopping suddenly. "There was a photo of Dr. Madsen, taken in her younger days. It's funny, but I could swear she was wearing a pendant just like yours." And she pointed to the Thor's hammer hanging on the silver chain around Margit's neck.

7

On Saturday morning Margit was feeling unusually cranky, even though she had only one small translation job to finish over the weekend. She was slow-moving and groggy after a restless night filled with alarming images that woke her up three times. But by eight a.m. she had only the vaguest recollection of her bad dreams.

She spent half an hour on the Nordic Track, trying to keep up with the rousing beat of "Spy in the House of Love" and the other tunes on Steve Winwood's new CD. She took a long hot shower, threw on some shorts and a t-shirt, and then set about making her morning latte. But she forgot the grinder was broken, and when she pushed the button, the lid flew off, ejecting coffee beans all over the kitchen.

"It's OK," she told her cat Gregor, who came dashing into the room when he heard her swearing loudly. "I'm just having one of those days."

Gregor looked up at her and blinked. Then he headed for his food dish on the floor next to the stove. He hunkered down and started purring contentedly as he crunched on the dry, fish-shaped nuggets.

Ten minutes later, Margit finally sat down at the dining-room table with a cup of instant espresso and two pieces of plain toast. She stared at the front page of the Local News section of Friday's *Seattle Times*, which was lying next to her placemat. She had stopped to buy a copy on her way home the night before. Renny's story about the death of the Danish doctor had made her curious. The article turned out to be quite brief, and it didn't say much more than what Renny had already reported. But it did mention that the woman was originally from Helsingør and had come to the U.S. in 1947. And Margit discovered that her friend was right—Gudrun Madsen was wearing a Thor's hammer in the old photo.

She stared at the picture for a moment, but then shrugged. So what? she told herself. Probably half the women in Denmark have pendants like that. Margit reread the noncommittal quote from Detective Tristano—"we'll know more after we've made a full investigation"—and then pushed the paper aside. She had to admit that she was feeling jittery about the meeting that was scheduled for one o'clock that afternoon.

After the art show, Renny had talked her into having a late Italian dinner. They both felt the need for some serious sustenance after hobnobbing with a crowd composed mainly of emaciated poseurs straight out of a Calvin Klein ad. When Margit got home around ten, she found the red light blinking on her answering machine. She turned up the volume and pushed the rewind button. Then she absent-mindedly picked up the latest newsletter from the American Translators Association. She was just scanning a tedious article about the use of the plural in modern Persian, when the voice coming from the machine stopped her short.

"This is Detective Tristano speaking. I wonder if you might be able to come down to the station around one o'clock tomorrow. You may have seen the news about the murder on Queen Anne. We've found some items that we assume are written in Danish, and we could use your help in translating them. Sorry to disturb your weekend, but it's rather urgent. You can leave a message with the duty officer at the precinct number. There's someone there twenty-four hours."

Margit wrote down the phone number and then played back the message twice. His tone of voice was certainly all business — even the apology for interrupting her weekend was curt. Not a hint that they even knew each other, let alone had spent several days roaming around Copenhagen together back in March.

Margit stared out the window as she sipped her coffee, but she hardly noticed the sparrows and chickadees squabbling over the last sunflower seeds in the bird feeder hanging from the Scotch pine.

What an odd trip that was, she thought, remembering how she had ended up actually enjoying the detective's company. He seemed less caustic and brusque than he was back in Seattle — definitely more relaxed. Maybe he just needed to get away from the pressures of his job more often.

"How about a tour of the city?" Tristano had suggested one day after they completed all the formal obligations that had brought them to Denmark in the first place.

Margit was surprised by his request, but she agreed to show him around Copenhagen, which she considered her second home. And Tristano turned out to be a surprisingly amenable sightseeing companion. Margit took him to see all the usual tourist attractions, including the famous statue of the Little Mermaid.

"She's been decapitated twice," said Margit, thinking that a police detective might be interested in the story about the theft of the statue's head.

But Tristano merely nodded and said, "She's a lot smaller than I thought she would be." Then they walked on toward the Freedom Museum, but it had already closed for the day.

One morning Margit even found herself showing the detective the reading room of the Royal Library where she had spent so many devoted hours doing literary research in her grad student days.

"Very impressive," Tristano said solemnly after surveying the vast, hushed hall filled with dedicated scholars hunched over long rows of desks. Margit gave him a sharp look to see if he meant to be sarcastic, but he seemed genuinely interested in the place. And it certainly was a magnificent reading room. Huge marble pillars reached up toward the vaulted ceiling high above, and thousands of books lined the walls—although most of the millions of volumes belonging to the collection were hidden away in the catacomblike depths of the building. Margit told the detective that she was one of the few people who had been privileged to work in the restricted inner sanctums. She was secretly pleased that he showed the proper reverence for the great library.

On the last day of their trip, Margit took Tristano to see the spectacular view from the top of the Round Tower, a seventeenth-century observatory built by King Christian IV in the middle of town. It was a brilliantly sunny day, but cold, with that biting Danish wind that could slice through even the thickest coat.

As they strolled around the deserted rooftop and Margit described all the points of interest, she surreptitiously studied the tall, dark-haired man at her side. Over lunch, after a few potent shots of Jubilæums aquavit, the normally close-mouthed detective had actually volunteered a few tidbits of personal information.

She now knew that he was thirty-four, only six years younger than she was. His youthful, athletic appearance had fooled her into thinking he was still in his late twenties. He grew up in the North Beach section of San Francisco, the eldest of a large Italian family. And to his mother's deep regret, he was still unmarried. He had been a Seattle homicide detective for four years.

That's as much as Tristano had been willing to reveal about himself, even in a slightly intoxicated state.

"What does the 'A' stand for?" Margit asked as they shivered in the brisk wind blowing across the Round Tower. The detective was shading his eyes from the bright sun and staring off into the distance, trying to catch a glimpse of the Swedish coastline.

"What did you say?" he asked, turning to look at her.

"The 'A' on your business card. It says 'Detective A. Tristano.' What does it stand for?"

A hint of embarrassment crept into his voice as he replied, "Alessandro. My mother likes extravagant names. But everyone just calls me Alex."

At that moment a strand of hair came loose from Margit's ponytail and blew into her face. Tristano spontaneously reached over to brush the lock out of her eyes, and then he did something even more unexpected. He leaned close and kissed her. It surprised them both.

A sharp meow pierced Margit's reverie, and she bent down to pet Gregor as he rubbed against the leg of her chair. He wanted to go out. "OK, in a minute," she said. "I just want to finish my breakfast."

She drank the rest of her espresso, remembering that when

she got back to Seattle, she hadn't been able to resist telling Renny about the kiss.

"Girl, I told you that man was loony about you," said Renny. "So what happened then?"

"Nothing," said Margit. "Nothing else happened. Really."

Renny had given her a skeptical look but refrained from asking any more questions. The only thing she said was, "So call him up. Don't you wait another minute. Call that man up."

But Margit couldn't make herself call him. There was Joe to consider, after all. And besides, she didn't know how she felt about dating a younger man. So she waited too long, and now it was too late. They were back on formal terms again.

"Come on, Gregor," said Margit, getting up. "Let's go feed the critters."

She filled a glass measuring cup with millet and sunflower seeds for the songbirds. She added a handful of hazelnuts on top for the Steller's jay that frequented her yard, and five or six walnuts for the squirrels. Then Margit went out the back door, with Gregor trotting along beside her, his black fur gleaming in the sun.

She had a few hours left to work on the kids' website she was translating from Norwegian, and then she would have to head for the police department downtown. She wondered why the detective couldn't just fax over the documents for her to translate. It would make it a lot easier for everybody.

As Margit filled the bird feeder, a tune kept running through her mind, and finally she realized what it was — that catchy Nick Lowe song: "Half a Boy and Half a Man."

8

At 12:55 Margit set her black canvas bag on the conveyor belt and then stepped through the metal detector at the security checkpoint just inside the entrance of the Public Safety Building.

"Can you tell me how to get to the homicide department?" she asked the silver-haired marshal standing nearby. He gave her a doubtful look, so she told him, "I have an appointment with Detective Tristano." To her annoyance, she could feel her face turning crimson. The man smiled and pointed out the appropriate elevator.

When the doors closed, Margit pushed the button and popped a peppermint Lifesaver into her mouth.

God, why am I so nervous? she thought, dropping her heavy bag to the floor. She had brought along her thick Dansk-Engelsk dictionary, just in case she needed to look something up. Fluency in a language didn't guarantee that she would be able to translate every single word she encountered, and it was always best to be prepared.

When Margit got off the elevator and was directed to the homicide department, she was surprised to find that the main area was divided up into cubicles, like any other modern office. She counted six spacious cubicles, each containing two desks and the usual office paraphernalia: telephones, computers, printers, and file cabinets. There were stacks of folders and paperwork everywhere. The place seemed remarkably quiet, but maybe that's because it was a Saturday. A phone rang three times, and Margit could hear the low drone of a few male voices conversing, but everything was much more calm and orderly than she had imagined.

You've been watching too many reruns of "Cagney & Lacey," she told herself as she shifted her canvas bag to her other hand.

"Ms. Andersson?" queried a familiar voice on her right. "Over here."

Margit turned to see Detective Tristano, nattily dressed in a cream-colored suit, gesturing to her from the entrance to one of the cubicles.

"Thanks for coming," he said, as she followed him into the space, where two wooden desks stood facing each other. "This is my partner, Ed Silikov."

Margit shook hands with the balding police detective, who politely stood up to greet her before going back to jabbing at his computer keyboard with two fingers. He was stockier than Tristano and much older—maybe in his mid-fifties—but there was a certain similarity to the two men that Margit ascribed to their meticulous attire and grooming. Silikov was wearing gold wire-rimmed glasses and a double-breasted gray suit that gave him the look of a banker.

Margit sat down on the proffered chair, hoping that her disappointment wasn't too obvious. It hadn't occurred to her that

Tristano might have a partner. Somehow she had thought they would have time alone.

"I take it that you've read about the case?"

"Yes, I have," said Margit, matching the detective's professional tone.

"Then you know that we're dealing with the murder of a seventy-six-year-old retired doctor, originally from Denmark. She was apparently pushed to her death from the bedroom window of her fifth-floor condominium on the west slope of Queen Anne."

"How do you know she was pushed?"

"Good question," said Silikov, looking up from his computer and giving Margit a nod. "That's always the first thing to consider in this type of case: Did the victim jump? Did she fall accidentally? Or was she pushed?

"There were no witnesses to her fall, and the people across the street were having a loud party, so nobody in the neighborhood heard anything. The medical examiner found a faint bruise on the victim's neck that might indicate an attempted strangulation. And in that case, the victim probably knew her attacker. But there were no other obvious marks on the body, so the M.E. bagged up her hands to check for tissue samples under her fingernails later. We don't have the results back yet."

Margit swallowed hard, as the details of the woman's death became all too vivid, but she tried to maintain a carefully neutral expression. She didn't want these two men to think her squeamish.

Tristano was leaning back in his chair, stroking his neatly trimmed mustache, obviously deferring to the greater experience of his partner.

"The first patrol officers on the scene found the door to her apartment locked," Silikov continued. "But when we entered the place later through the balcony, we found the safety chain wasn't fastened on the front door and the deadbolt wasn't locked either. Anyone could have turned the simple button-lock in the doorknob and then pulled the door shut behind them. We ruled out robbery, since nothing seemed to be disturbed or missing, and the victim had well over five hundred dollars in her handbag on the kitchen table."

"But I thought the paper said there were signs of a struggle," said Margit.

"Yes, but they can be quite subtle when you're dealing with elderly victims, who usually don't have the strength to fight back. In this case, we found a wicker chair overturned in the bedroom and a glass of water spilled on the nightstand. There was also a small broken planter box lying under the body. From the looks of the marks left on the windowsill, the planter had been there a long time. It seems highly unlikely that a woman intent on jumping to her death would choose a window with a planter box in it. Especially when she's got a nice balcony just down the hall."

"We also found this near the body," said Tristano suddenly, leaning forward to hand Margit two photographs.

She involuntarily shut her eyes, not prepared for whatever gruesome image the pictures might hold.

But when she forced herself to look at the photos, there was no sign of the corpse or any other horrific sight. Margit was staring at close-ups of what looked like two small copper coins against white backdrops. One was engraved with a pair of ears and underneath were the English words "The walls have ears." The other coin showed a man walking forward, bent low from the weight of two wooden doors he was carrying on his back. In Danish it said *"Gaa stille med dørene."*

"You found these coins near the body?" asked Margit.

"They're actually two sides of the same coin," said the detective. "It was lying only a few inches away from the victim's right hand. Can you tell us what it says under the guy carrying the doors?"

"Yes, it's in Danish all right. It says literally 'walk quietly with the doors,' but that doesn't make any sense, so I assume it's an idiom. Let me look it up."

Margit pulled the heavy dictionary out of her bag and placed it on her lap. She found the lengthy entry for the word "*dør*," and ran her forefinger down the column until she found what she was searching for. "Here it is," she said. "It means 'shut the doors softly' but the figurative meaning is to 'lie low, watch your step, be discreet.'"

Margit closed the dictionary and looked up. "I guess that's just about the same thing as the English inscription. They both sound like some kind of warning, don't they?"

"Any idea what it might signify? Have you ever seen this type of coin before?"

"No," said Margit, shaking her head and handing the photos back to Tristano. "I don't know what it means."

"OK. Take a look at this," said Detective Silikov, sliding a sheet of typing paper across his desk toward Margit. "We picked up these words from the impressions left on a notepad next to the victim's telephone. The actual note was gone, but we think we got all the letters right. Can you make any sense out of them?"

Margit picked up the paper, scanned the Danish words, and then translated the cursory letter for the detectives.

"Dear Muninn," she read. "There's nothing I can do to stop her. She insists on coming. Can you catch the 9:25? I'll wait for you at the bookstore. Huginn."

"Hmm," said Tristano. "Is Muninn a man or a woman's

name? And what about the signature? Does it mean anything? Is it some kind of Danish nickname that the doctor might have used?"

"First of all, Muninn is not a man *or* a woman. And neither is Huginn," said Margit, enjoying the perplexed look she received from both detectives. "The Nordic god Odin, who is sometimes compared to the god Mercury, had two ravens named Muninn and Huginn. It was their job to go out into the world and bring back information. One stood for Memory and the other for Thought. If Dr. Madsen wrote this note, I have no idea why she would use such a cryptic signature."

Silikov asked Margit to read the letter again, as he typed the translation into his computer. Then he handed her five more photographs. The picture on top showed a desk calendar—the kind often used as a blotter, with an entire month on one large page. Each of the other photos showed a close-up of a quarter of the calendar. Margit squinted at the words scribbled into the spaces allocated for each day of July.

"Here," said Tristano, "this should make it easier." And he handed her a magnifying glass.

Margit accepted it reluctantly. This wasn't the first time that she realized her eyesight was getting bad. She was going to have to break down and buy herself a pair of reading glasses. A sure sign of encroaching decrepitude, in her opinion.

She began translating the Danish words she was able to make out on the calendar. "July 1st: Dentist, 3:15. July 4th: Party at Kirsten's. July 8th: Call plumber."

Suddenly Margit stopped reading and passed the photo and magnifying glass back to Tristano, saying, "Take a look at Thursday, July 10th."

"What about it?" he asked.

"Doesn't that look like the drawing of a flower, maybe even a rose? And underneath it says '☆1557/1205.'"

"Yes, we're not sure what that means."

"Well, I know exactly what it means," said Margit, "Star Air flight 1557 is scheduled to arrive at Sea-Tac at 12:05 on Thursdays. I go out there every week to act as the interpreter. And I'll bet you ten bucks that Dr. Madsen was going to meet a passenger named Rosa—Rosa Nørgaard."

"And who is that?"

"The woman who died at the airport on July 10th. They said she died of a heart attack, but now I'm starting to think that I was right all along—I think she actually died of fright."

9

I 'll have a double iced latte," said Margit to the cheerful teenager who was taking orders at the counter in the aromatic
SBC coffee shop at Westlake Center. "And two molasses cookies." She had skipped lunch, too nervous to eat anything before
her meeting with the detective. As she walked through town after leaving the police department, she had quickly devoured the
apple and crackers in her bag, but she was still hungry.

Margit sat down on a nearby bench outside and surveyed
the crowds of weekend shoppers. Westlake Center had originally
been designed as a small downtown plaza, with no traffic allowed on the one-block stretch of Pine Street that bisected the
area. For several years it had been a popular urban park, offering a spacious haven for vendors, street musicians, jugglers, and
office workers relaxing outdoors on their lunch hour. But a local
department store had decided that the pedestrian mall was detri-
mental to its business, and the company had used its political
clout to reopen the street to cars. The lazy ambience of the plaza
had vanished overnight.

Margit glanced up at the sky as the sun slipped behind the clouds. It was still a pleasant 72 degrees, but it looked as if the prediction of a light afternoon shower might prove to be true.

The interview with the two detectives had not ended as Margit had hoped. While Silikov typed up what she could tell him about the death of Rosa Nørgaard, Tristano dialed the number of the Sea-Tac police. He was still on the phone when Margit was ready to leave. He paused long enough to say "Thanks for your help," and then went back to his phone conversation. It was obviously not the right time for any personal remarks, such as the apology Margit had intended to offer for not getting back to him when he left a message on her answering machine well over three months ago.

Detective Silikov was on his way out, and he offered to escort Margit down to the building entrance.

"I'm surprised that you were willing to tell me so much about the case," she said as they waited for the elevator.

"There's usually no reason to keep most things secret," said Silikov. "We don't need to broadcast all the details in the media, but when we're working on a homicide, we need lots of help to solve the case. And it's especially useful if we get the help of someone like yourself who knows the ethnic community involved. Sometimes there are specific cultural customs or traits that can give us a lead.

"I had a case recently where a man was found dead with his genitals cut off. The murderer turned out to be Hispanic and we found out that the mutilation was a macho thing—an act of revenge against the victim who had been fooling around with the perpetrator's wife."

Margit was glad the elevator arrived at that moment. She wasn't sure she wanted to hear any more gory details. And she wondered what her Chicana friend Barbro would say about that type of male vengeance.

"Isn't your job kind of depressing?" she couldn't help blurting out as they descended to the ground floor.

Silikov shook his head. "It's stressful, because of course you want to solve the case as quickly as possible. And you're in contact with the victim's family members, so you want to do it right for them. But it's not depressing. After an investigation is over, you just let the case go and move on to the next one."

"Don't they ever give you nightmares?"

"Well, there are a couple of kids who were murdered that I still remember," Silikov admitted. "And sometimes I see kids out on the street and I think about them. But otherwise, no—you just have to let the cases go."

"How can you stand to be around dead bodies all the time?" asked Margit, unable to contain her curiosity.

"The percentage of time you actually spend with the body is very small. Maybe an hour or so at the scene, and then you watch the autopsy—although these days, you're not even there for the whole thing. You just come in after the body's been all cleaned up to examine the wounds. You might spend three weeks on a case, but only a couple of hours with the dead person. The rest of the time you're talking to witnesses and family members, and you're out gathering evidence."

"Why would anyone want to be a homicide detective in the first place?" Margit asked, thinking about Tristano.

"It's important work," replied Silikov solemnly. Then he grinned and added, "Besides, it's exciting. It becomes your whole life."

As they stepped out of the elevator on the first floor, Silikov stopped to straighten his tie and flick a speck of dust off his sleeve.

"Take Alex, for instance," he said. "He's one of our best young detectives. In another year or so, he'll be at the top of his game. It takes five or six years to really know what you're doing. Homicide detectives are all perfectionists to start with, and it's very exacting and demanding work. You have to do everything right. Anyone who takes this kind of job usually stays with it for a long time. Look at me—I've been doing this now for over fifteen years."

He held open the door for Margit, and then shook her hand as they said goodbye in front of the building.

"Well, thanks for your help, Ms. Andersson. By the way, I heard you had a nice time sightseeing in Copenhagen." And Silikov gave her a wink before he strode off down the street.

As she finished the second molasses cookie, Margit wondered what else Tristano might have told his partner about the trip to Denmark.

"Mind if I sit here?"

Margit looked up to see a slender young woman in a sleeveless green dress standing in front of her. She was holding a steaming cup of coffee in her hand.

"No, go ahead."

"You don't recognize me, do you?" said the woman, smiling as she sat down on the bench.

Margit gave her a closer look. She had blue eyes, long golden hair pulled back into a thick French braid, and a flawless fair complexion. There was no doubt about her Scandinavian heritage, and Margit thought she had caught a hint of a Norwegian accent in her English. The lilting intonation of spoken

Norwegian always reminded her of a chirping bird. It was much livelier than the regular rise and fall of Swedish or the flat monotone of Danish. Norwegian could make even a gruff-looking man sound irrepressibly perky.

"Nobody recognizes me when I'm not in uniform," explained the woman. "I'm a flight attendant for those summer charters that Star Air has been handling. I've seen you out at the airport a few times. You're the interpreter, aren't you?"

"Yes," said Margit. "Oh, that's right, I remember seeing you too." And she pictured the blonde woman wearing the standard navy-blue uniform that all airlines seemed to have adopted. Uniforms did exactly what they were intended to do—they made the wearer anonymous, blanking out all trace of individuality. Brian had told Margit that when he put on his uniform he stepped right into his airline persona. His wife said even his voice sounded different. The transformation was so complete that he had trouble switching into any other mode.

One day a passenger checking in at the ticket counter had scrutinized Brian's name tag and then exclaimed, "Aren't you the famous translator? Didn't you translate *Sinister Cinnamon*?"

Brian told Margit that he was thoroughly shocked. He felt as if he had been unmasked, and he suffered a panic-stricken moment of sheer schizophrenia. Part of him was flattered by the recognition, and he had a sudden urge to talk about books. But the force of his uniform quickly took over, and he responded with a terse: "Yes, I did." Then he was once again playing the role of assistant station manager, telling the passenger, "We're going to have to check your garment bag. It's too big to fit in the overhead bin."

Margit introduced herself to the woman sitting beside her.

"Ingrid Sæterstad," replied the flight attendant, shaking Margit's hand. "Do you speak Norwegian?"

"Danish and Swedish."

"Ah, well... That's OK. We can speak English."

Margit stopped herself from making a snide remark. It always annoyed her that most Scandinavians preferred to communicate with each other in English. In her opinion, anyone who spoke one of the three major Nordic languages should be able to understand the other two. All it took was a little patience and flexibility.

Danish, Norwegian, and Swedish were close enough in syntax and vocabulary to be mutually understandable. Modern Icelandic was another story, since over the centuries it had remained staunchly loyal to its Old Norse origins, while the other three languages had come under the influence of German, French, and English. And Finnish, of course, was in a class by itself. It didn't even belong to the family of Indo-European languages. Estonian was the only language that came close, although historically they were both related to Hungarian. But that didn't mean that Finns could understand Hungarians, or vice versa.

Margit acknowledged that the three Nordic languages certainly had their differences in both pronunciation and meaning. The classic example was the word "*rolig*," which meant "calm" in Danish and Norwegian, but "funny" in Swedish. And "*frokost*" meant "lunch" in Danish, but "breakfast" in Norwegian. That could lead to some significant misunderstandings. But on the whole, Margit couldn't see that the differences were much greater than those between the dialects of English spoken in Texas and Scotland. Maybe her perspective had become slightly warped after working as a translator for so many years.

"I feel bad about that woman who died," said Ingrid. "She was sitting in my section on the plane, but I didn't have a chance to talk to her much. I had my hands full with some rowdy agricultural students from Horsens who were coming over here to take a seminar in Pullman."

"Did Fru Nørgaard happen to tell you why she was coming to Seattle?"

"No, I have no idea. The police asked me that too." Ingrid put her hand up to her mouth to hide a yawn.

"Jet lag?" asked Margit sympathetically. The nine-hour time difference between Seattle and Scandinavia made travel between the two destinations a disorienting experience. After a European trip, it always took Margit at least a week to feel like her body had readjusted and was back on a normal schedule.

"Yes," said Ingrid, "but that's just part of the job. We never feel totally rested, even with a two- or three-day layover between flights. When I first started flying, I had this strange idea that I would be immune to the effects of jet lag and other occupational hazards. I was excited about going off to all different parts of the world, and I didn't want to believe the warnings I heard from older flight attendants—about insomnia, noisy hotel rooms, bad food, and a bone-deep fatigue that's impossible to shake. Not to mention the stress of dealing with weird passengers."

Ingrid took a sip of her coffee. "My friends are always telling me horror stories. Like about the invasion of the Rajneeshies a few years back. Remember those cult members who all wore pink and red clothes? They filled up all the charters flying into Seattle, on their way to that little town in Oregon where their guru had settled. I guess their behavior on board the flights was sometimes really outrageous. They danced and sang in the aisles, and they even made love in the seats. I'm glad I wasn't flying this route back then."

"What a nightmare," said Margit.

"Uh-huh. But the worst thing about the job is the wear and tear on your body. Some of my colleagues have even developed carpal tunnel syndrome from pouring coffee all day long."

"You're kidding."

"No, really. Just think about hoisting a heavy coffee pot three or four hundred times a day. That kind of repetitive motion is just as hard on your wrist as typing at a computer. The airline I work for finally hired a designer to create a coffee pot that would put less stress on the hand. Anyway, after five years on the job, I feel tired most of the time. I guess I've lost some of my enthusiasm too."

"So it's not as much fun as it used to be?"

"Well, I still love to fly," said Ingrid, "but I have to admit that some days I cringe when the first passenger walks on board. It's not as easy as you think to be pleasant and polite all the time, especially when you're cooped up with two or three hundred people at 30,000 feet."

"When do you go back?"

"Tomorrow. I work the charter to Amsterdam, then dead-head to Copenhagen. I get Tuesday and Wednesday off before I'm due back here in Seattle on Thursday."

"Deadhead?" said Margit, thinking suddenly of a Grateful Dead concert she had gone to in the seventies.

"Sorry. That's airline talk. It means flying off-duty as a passenger—to get back to the city where you're stationed."

Ingrid finished her coffee and crumpled up the paper cup in her hand. "Too bad I have to leave so soon. My aunt invited me to the Pan-Scandinavian picnic tomorrow, but I'm going to have to miss it."

"You have relatives in Seattle?" asked Margit.

"Yes, one branch of my father's family immigrated to the

U.S. back in the twenties. You might know my aunt. She's very active in the Scandinavian community here. I get the impression she knows everybody. Her name is Toril Christensen."

"I've heard of her," said Margit, nodding. "But I don't think we've ever met."

Margit occasionally went to lectures at the Danish Foundation and she had seen some good exhibits at the Nordic Heritage Museum, but she seldom attended functions sponsored by the traditional Scandinavian clubs. They tended to cater to the more conservative interests of immigrants who belonged to her parents' generation.

Suddenly Margit thought about what Detective Silikov had said: "It's especially useful if we get the help of someone like yourself who knows the ethnic community involved."

Scandinavians were generally a reserved and taciturn lot; they didn't readily welcome strangers into their circles. No one would purposely withhold information from the police, but they might not mention some bit of gossip that could prove useful. Margit's Scandinavian background gave her an inside edge.

Maybe I'll just drop by that picnic, she thought. It would only take her a couple of hours to finish the translation job she was working on, so then she'd have Sunday free. Maybe she could find out something about Dr. Madsen. Or even Rosa Nørgaard. Margit decided to have a talk with Toril Christensen.

"Where's the picnic going to be held?" she asked.

"It's at Lincoln Park," said Ingrid. "And this time I hear they've even invited the Finns."

10

Margit slammed down the phone and picked up her day-pack from the floor. That was the third time someone had called in the past few days and then hung up as soon as she answered. This time she could swear that she heard breathing on the other end of the line as she repeated "Hello? Hello?" Then there was a sharp click and the connection went dead.

People are just too rude, she thought as she went out the front door, locking it behind her.

Margit took her shiny blue touring bicycle out of the garage, strapped on her bike helmet, and adjusted her sunglasses. Then she rode off down the street, calling "See you later" to Gregor, who was lounging in the shade next to the fence. He stared after her for a moment and then went back to licking his fur. Fortunately, he had never gotten into the habit of following Margit when she went out for a bike ride.

If she was on foot, Gregor would happily accompany her for several blocks, until he reached the invisible boundary of his feline territory. Then he would get nervous and start howling, the way he did in the car when he had to go to the vet. If Margit wanted to continue her walk, she would have to turn around and put Gregor back in the house first.

It was a perfect day for a picnic. Sunny and warm, with a light breeze and not a cloud in the sky. Seattle was having an unusually hot and dry summer. Margit kept telling herself to enjoy it instead of dwelling on the probable reasons for the climatic change. She had recently translated several ominous articles about global warming, but she didn't want to think about that today.

Margit pedaled slowly along the quiet residential streets of West Seattle, heading for Lincoln Park, which was only a few miles away. The Scandinavian picnic wouldn't really get started until two o'clock, so she had plenty of time. Besides, she was still feeling a little sluggish from the spinach and mushroom omelette she'd had for breakfast at the Cedar Café.

When Margit pushed open the door to the popular eatery in the Admiral District at nine that morning, she had found the place already packed. Sunday was always busy because Bob—who was both owner and cook—put all of his culinary artistry into creating breakfast specials that were offered only on the weekend.

Renny was clearing off a table in the back of the café when she saw Margit come in. She waved the dishcloth she was holding and redirected several other customers to another table in order to save the choice window seat for her friend.

"What are you doing bussing tables?" asked Margit as she sat down. Renny was the café's expert barista, working several days a week behind the counter at the deluxe espresso machine. But she had recently cut back her hours to devote more time to her painting—thanks to a grant from the Puget Arts Foundation.

"Hi, kiddo. We're short-handed today. Nick didn't show up again, so we're all doing double duty. But I really need a break—I'll join you in a minute."

Margit was halfway through her omelette by the time Renny came back, setting her cup of Ruby Mist tea on the table as she sat down. Then she snagged a piece of toast from Margit's plate.

"Some days I'd give anything for a cup of coffee," said Renny with a sigh, "even though I know it's not worth it." Several years back she had been forced to give up all forms of caffeine because it aggravated an inner ear imbalance she had developed. Even chocolate made her impossibly dizzy. Everyone claimed that Renny made the best latte in town, but few people realized that she couldn't drink coffee herself, not even decaf.

"So what's this about a Scandinavian picnic?"

"It's at Lincoln Park this year," said Margit. "I thought I'd ride my bike over. Want to stop by after you get off work?"

"What kind of food are they going to have?"

"Well, it's a potluck, so the Norwegians will probably serve flatbread and *lefse*, with herring salad and marinated smelt."

"What? No *lutefisk*?"

"No, that's only at Christmastime," said Margit with a grimace. She had never acquired a taste for the pale, lye-cured cod, which many people considered a delicacy. "The Danes will have open-faced sandwiches with things like liver paste and pickled beets, or sliced roast beef topped with *sky*—that's jellied marrow. Some of the older Danes might bring *fedtemad*, which is bacon drippings spread on rye bread. The Swedes will serve meatballs and their usual favorite, 'Jansson's Temptation,' a casserole made of potatoes, onions, and anchovies. And I hear the Finns are coming this year, so I expect they'll bring liver hash and cucumber soup."

"My God, Margit—I think I'll pass. That's not exactly my idea of picnic food. And I know you sometimes eat fish, but it doesn't sound like there'll be much else on the menu for a vegetarian like you."

"I know. That's why I'm having a big breakfast. But the desserts should be good."

"How come you're so keen on going to this thing, anyway? I thought you didn't like these local Scando events."

"Oh, I thought I'd just have a talk with a few people there," said Margit, lowering her glance to her plate.

"This doesn't have something to do with a murder investigation, does it?" asked Renny suspiciously. Margit had told her about her visit to the police department the day before. "I hope you're not thinking of getting mixed up in detective work again. Remember what happened the last time?"

"Stop worrying. I just thought I'd ask a couple of people whether they knew Dr. Madsen or the woman who died at the airport. That's all."

"I guess that would give you a good excuse to call up a certain Alex Tristano, wouldn't it?"

Margit fervently denied any such motive. But now, as she rode her bike along the shoreline path below the park and looked out at the sparkling water of the Sound, she had to admit that Renny was right. If she found out anything at all, it *would* give her a good reason to call up the detective.

She shook her head and told herself to stop acting like a lovesick teenager. She was probably just suffering from post-breakup panic, when loneliness could easily prompt ill-advised attachments. That's what happened after she divorced her husband back in 1987. The marriage had lasted only three years, but the breakup was still traumatic. And Margit had gone through several unsuitable lovers in rapid succession until she realized that living alone might have its advantages. When the last unwanted boyfriend finally decamped, she told Renny with disgust, "I'd rather see that guy's heel than his toe—to use a good Danish expression."

But Joe was different. She had even considered moving to the Southwest for his sake. Now she didn't know how she felt about him. But she thought it might be a good idea to heed the warning on that copper coin and "lie low" for a while.

"Hi, Margit! I didn't know you were coming to the picnic."

Margit turned her head to the left to see Lars and Derek sitting on a nearby bench. She waved, then hopped off her bike and walked over toward them. Lars Ekström was another Scandinavian translator who did freelance work for the Koivisto Translation Agency.

"Soaking up some sun?" Margit asked her colleague.

"Yup. Thought we'd better take a walk along the water before we attack the *smörgåsbord*. I want Derek to try out all the different dishes." Ever since they had moved in together, Lars was always trying to introduce his partner to the Scandinavian traditions that he had grown up with. Derek Cameron was an amiable man who seemed to take it all in stride, even agreeing to enroll in a beginning Swedish course. But he once confided to Margit that he found the Scandinavian cultures fundamentally gloomy and restrained. Being intimately familiar with the customs of the North, Margit could only agree with his assessment.

"Everyone at the picnic is talking about the Queen Anne murder," said Lars.

So Margit told him about the connection between the victim and Rosa Nørgaard. She also mentioned her interview with the police and the coin with the odd inscriptions, but Lars had no idea what they might mean.

"Do you happen to know Toril Christensen?" Margit asked him. "I thought I'd find out if she knew Dr. Madsen."

"I'm sure she did. She knows just about everybody. If you go up on the bluff to picnic area number four, you'll find her supervising the food tables. She's wearing an apron with a Norwegian flag on it."

Ten minutes later Margit propped her bike next to a tree, hung her helmet over the handlebars, and slowly made her way through the swarms of picnicking families. A cheer rose up from the crowd of spectators watching the nearby soccer game, but Margit couldn't tell if the roar of approval was meant for the Danish or Swedish team. On the other side of the soccer field, ten or twelve Norwegians were folkdancing to a screechy tape recording of fiddle music. And the Finns were in the midst of preparations for one of their favorite events: the wife-carrying races.

Margit found Toril Christensen standing behind a long row of picnic tables covered with a vast array of homemade Scandinavian foods. She was a plump woman in her late fifties, and she was pleased to hear that Margit had met her niece the day before. They chatted for a few minutes about airline companies and other inconsequential matters before Margit brought up the subject of Gudrun Madsen's death.

"Did you know her personally?" Margit asked.

"Oh yes. She was our family doctor when my kids were small. Of course, I haven't seen her in years. Not since her husband died and she stopped coming to any of the Scandinavian get-togethers."

"Do you know if she was friends with a woman named Rosa Nørgaard?"

"No, never heard of her. But I don't think Gudrun had a lot of friends. She lived alone, and her only daughter moved to Missoula a long time ago."

"Did she have any enemies?"

"Heavens, no," exclaimed the woman, shaking her head. "Why would anyone want to hurt Gudrun Madsen? She was such a quiet, unassuming person. And so good with children. She was a very good doctor, you know. Isn't it terrible? How could something like this happen?"

"I read in the paper that she emigrated from Helsingør in 1947," said Margit, trying a different tack.

"Yes, she came here after the war. Finished up her medical training in Denmark and then married Niels Madsen, a Danish-American businessman. I think he was actually a distant cousin on her mother's side. No, maybe he was related to her father's side of the family. If I remember right, they were originally farmers from Lolland—"

Margit interrupted Toril before she got lost in the maze of family genealogy, which was a favorite topic among second- and third-generation Scandinavian-Americans.

"Have you ever seen a copper coin inscribed with the words 'the walls have ears'?"

"Why yes—yes, I have," said Toril, giving Margit a look of surprise. "My father had a coin like that. He was a big history buff, and he collected memorabilia from World War II. I remember that particular coin because as a kid I liked the picture of the two ears."

"Do you know what the inscription means?"

"Well, my father told me that those coins were made in 1944. The idea came from a group of students who sold them for five kroner each, to benefit the efforts of the Danish freedom fighters during the German occupation of the country. He said that the coins were passed from one person to another as a warning that an informer was in their midst."

Toril paused for a moment, and then added, "And as a matter of fact, I remember my father saying that those coins were especially favored by doctors and other hospital personnel. Does this have something to do with Dr. Madsen's death?"

"It might," said Margit warily, not sure how much she should tell Toril about the case, since she didn't really know her. She decided not to say anything about the note with the cryptic signature.

"Well, if you want to know more about the war years in Denmark," continued Toril, "you should go talk to Egon. Egon Kirkeby. He was right in the thick of things, you know. He was in the Danish underground."

11

The shrill sound of the telephone woke Margit up at seven thirty on Monday morning. On the fifth ring, she finally rolled out of bed with a groan and ran down the hall to her study. She must have turned off her answering machine by mistake. She was going to be furious if someone had yanked her away from her beauty sleep, only to hang up on her without saying a word. And for once she was having a pleasant dream that she would have liked to finish. Something about sailing across the Sound with dolphins leaping alongside the boat.

"Hello?" she growled.

"Margit? It's Lars."

His voice was so scratchy and hoarse that it was barely recognizable.

"You sound awful. What happened?"

"My allergies are acting up, and I guess I've come down with a summer cold too. It probably didn't help that we went swimming in Lake Washington last night. Listen, I'm sorry to call you this early, but the agency just sent me a Swedish job to translate, and I wonder if you could take it instead. My head feels like it's got a jackhammer inside, and I know I won't be able to concentrate. The job's due at the end of the day, of course. Typical."

"OK," said Margit, running her hand through her hair and yawning. "Sure. How many words? And what's the topic?"

"Looks like about 3,000 words. Documents dealing with some kind of clinical trials for a hospital."

"Oh, lovely. Just the way I want to spend my day. It won't be nearly as much fun as that list of prohibited words that I just sent off as part of the Norwegian website for kids that I was translating."

"Prohibited words?" croaked Lars.

"Uh-huh. They didn't want kids to be typing in words like 'fuck' and 'shit' when they're playing the interactive games on the website, so they decided to program in a list of banned words that wouldn't be accepted. I wish I could see Liisa's face when she edits that job. Do you think she's going to quibble about my translation of the word '*pikk*'?"

Lars laughed. Liisa Koivisto was the owner of the translation agency which kept both Margit and Lars busy most of the time—they certainly couldn't complain of any lack of work. But she was a perfectionist who could drive them crazy with her nitpicking. And since she was a Finn who could also read Swedish, Danish, and Norwegian, she always took it upon herself to double-check their work personally before sending it off to the client.

"All right. Go ahead and fax over the documents," Margit told Lars. "I guess I owe you one after you saved my neck on that last medical job."

Fortunately for her, Lars had agreed to edit a difficult translation she had recently done for a Swedish pharmaceutical company. To Margit's embarrassment, he discovered that she had misread the phrase "*ett fåtal tillfällen*" (meaning "a few cases") and mistaken it for "*ett fatalt tillfälle*" (meaning "one fatal case"). She really was going to have to get those reading glasses. But at least Lars caught the error before the translation reached Liisa's critical eye.

Margit sat down at her desk and switched on the computer. She would have to wait to read her email until the pages of the translation job finished spewing out of her fax machine. Her Internet connection used the same phone line. Margit pulled up a game of Taipei instead and began lazily clicking on the matching tiles. She was still half asleep, since she had ended up talking to Egon Kirkeby until almost midnight.

Toril had wasted no time in putting Margit in touch with her friend on Sunday afternoon. She marched right over to the enclave of Finnish picnickers and borrowed a cell phone to call him up. "All the Finns have Nokia cell phones these days," she told Margit, sounding impressed, as she dialed Egon Kirkeby's number. When she got through to him, Toril explained that she was at the picnic with a young woman who had some questions about the war years, and she knew that Egon would be the best person to talk to.

Then Margit took the phone, and she found herself speaking to a man with a heavy Danish accent. When she told him about the copper coin, there was a long silence on the phone, and then he invited her to come over for a talk. "How about eight o'clock tonight?" he said. "Things should be quiet here by then."

"Fine," said Margit, a little taken aback by the whole turn of events. But she wrote down his Crown Hill address before handing the cell phone back to Toril, who returned it to its proper owner.

Half an hour later Margit rode her bike back home, took a cool shower, and turned on all the fans. Her small two-bedroom house was stifling after baking in the hot afternoon sun. She put on a Temptations CD, programmed the player to start with "I Wish It Would Rain," and turned up the volume. Like most true Northerners, Margit felt anesthetized by hot weather. She loved the extra hours of sunlight in the summertime, but not the heat. She felt most comfortable when the temperature dropped to around 60 degrees and she could put on her favorite outfit: an old pair of jeans and a loose sweater.

Gregor was restlessly roaming around the living room, rubbing his cheek on all the furniture legs. It was his way of saying that he wanted dinner. He never rubbed against people's legs to get attention, the way most cats did. Margit always assumed that he must have been kicked as a kitten. He was also scared of brooms.

"Lucky for you that I took you in," she told him, bending down to pet his bulky head as he purred loudly. Gregor had begun showing up on Margit's porch a few years back, when the family next door blithely abandoned him and moved to Sedro Woolley.

They went into the kitchen together, and Margit opened a can of Kitty Stew—a special Sunday treat for Gregor. Then she fixed herself a small salad. She wasn't very hungry after gobbling down two pieces of Danish *Wienerbrød* and some Finnish *pulla* at the park, but she needed something besides sugar to keep her going.

At seven thirty Margit climbed into the driver's seat of her old Mazda and turned the key in the ignition. A horrible grinding noise issued from the engine, and it took three more nerve-shattering tries before the car finally started up. Everything seemed to be falling apart lately: her car, her relationship with Joe, her eyesight. And just last week she had been forced to buy a new washing machine when the old one suddenly died.

By the time Margit rang the doorbell at Egon Kirkeby's house, she was feeling hot and grumpy, and she wondered what she was doing there at all. But it turned out to be a most interesting visit.

"Come in, come in," said the short, wiry man who opened the door and gave Margit a brisk handshake. "So you're Toril's friend?"

"Well, not really," said Margit, "but I know her niece." This was a bit of an overstatement, but she was aware that personal connections were important to the older generation.

Egon Kirkeby looked like he was in his early seventies, with a weatherbeaten face and surprisingly thick, curly hair that was still a burnished gold. He had that boyish air about him that many Danish men never seemed to lose, no matter what their age. In some cases this was clearly a sign of emotional immaturity; in others it was a manifestation of personal charm and vitality. Egon turned out to belong to the latter group.

"My father and I were just having our evening coffee," he told Margit as he led the way to a cheerful living room, attractively furnished. An overstuffed sofa and matching armchairs upholstered in a flowery chintz fabric took up most of the space. An upright piano, its dark wood gleaming, stood in one corner. And the far wall was entirely covered with rows of blue-and-white porcelain plates—the kind that were issued each Christmas by the Royal Copenhagen company. Since the year was always incorporated into the design, Margit could see that the first plate dated back to 1950.

"That's quite a collection," she told her host, realizing that some of the older plates must be quite valuable by now.

"Yes," Egon said, with a smile. "It was my wife's hobby. She loved glass and porcelain. We have the Bing & Grøndahl plates in the dining room.

"She passed away a couple of years ago," he added, with a slight quiver to his voice. He looked as if he still couldn't quite believe that she was gone.

"I'm sorry to hear that," said Margit politely.

"*Hva'beha'r?*" grumbled a voice out of nowhere.

"It's all right, Father," said Egon in Danish, stepping in front of the armchair which stood with its back to the living room entrance. "Remember I told you that we were going to have a guest tonight?"

Margit moved around to Egon's side and found herself looking down at a wizened old man huddled against the cushions of the high-backed armchair. It was clear that he had just woken up from a nap. His eyes were red-rimmed and watery, his white hair was sticking up, and the collar of his light-blue shirt was rumpled. In spite of the heat he was wearing a navy-blue knit vest with gold buttons, a dark brown suit, and a striped tie. His pale right hand was slowly stroking the fur of a gray cat curled up beside him.

"*Go' aften,*" said Margit, switching to Danish and introducing herself.

"You speak Danish?" asked Egon in surprise.

"Oh yes," she told him. "My mother is from Copenhagen."

Egon's father nodded to Margit, shook her hand, and then went back to petting the cat. "There's nothing as comforting as a tame animal," he murmured. "We're good friends, aren't we? We're the best of friends. And you always sit right next to me, don't you?"

"Father is ninety-two," whispered Egon to Margit in English

as she sat down on the other armchair and he took his place on the sofa. "I was hoping he might have gone off to bed by now, so we could talk in peace, but he'll probably nod out in a minute anyway." Egon poured coffee from a silver Georg Jensen pot into three delicate china cups. Then he offered Margit and his father butter cookies, which he had baked himself.

"Where did you come across that coin you were telling me about on the phone?" Egon asked Margit. He was speaking Danish again, out of consideration for his father, even though the old man didn't seem to be paying any attention to their conversation.

Margit told Egon about the coin found at the scene of Gudrun Madsen's death. She also decided to mention the cryptic note found in her apartment. It turned out that he had met the doctor and her husband a few times at Danish Brotherhood parties, but that was years ago. He had never heard of Rosa Nørgaard.

"Toril told me the coin was from the war years. She said it had something to do with the Danish resistance and that you were involved with the movement," said Margit.

"Yes, that's right. When the Germans invaded Denmark on April 9, 1940, I was just a naïve fourteen-year-old and as shocked as everybody else that we were suddenly an occupied country. But then I read Arne Sejr's leaflet 'The Dane's Ten Commandments,' and it changed my life. Even though I was only a kid, I knew I had to do something. I couldn't just sit back and watch the Germans take over."

"Who was Arne Sejr?" asked Margit.

"He was a student from Slagelse—an incredibly brave and enterprising young man who set up the Student Intelligence Service, or the 'S.I.' A nationwide network of high school and university students who started out by printing handbills that protested the occupation and urged people to resist. The group ended up getting involved in all kinds of illegal activities, including sabotage, intelligence work, and the transport of weapons. I became a messenger for the S.I., and later on I helped write and distribute the biweekly underground paper. By 1944 it had a circulation of nearly 75,000."

Egon poured himself another cup of coffee. "Funny how people's lives turn out," he said with a smile. "I ended up in the newspaper business myself, you know. Worked as a reporter for the *Seattle Times* for thirty-five years."

"How does the coin fit into the picture?" asked Margit, hoping to keep Egon from getting too sidetracked.

"Well, that was later, after things started heating up, and the Germans dropped all pretense of benign rule. When the general strikes erupted in August of 1943, the Nazis really started cracking down."

Egon's father suddenly cleared his throat and broke into the conversation. He stared straight across at Margit and said in a low voice, "I'm such an old man that I've been through two world wars. During the second one, King Christian X used to ride through the streets of Copenhagen every day on a big horse. Without an escort. Well, there was a man who followed him at a distance, carrying something. I think it might have been a hat."

Margit and Egon exchanged glances, trying not to laugh at this incongruous remark in an otherwise somber account. They let the old man continue without interrupting.

"And all of the Germans were so impressed with the king's proud bearing and his lack of fear, that they stood along the streets and raised their arms in the Nazi salute, the 'Heil Hitler.'" And the old man raised his own hand in the infamous gesture to illustrate his point.

"But the king would ride past them without a glimmer of acknowledgment. He would turn his head and look the other way."

Egon's father nodded a few times, and then started telling the same story over again, with exactly the same wording, the same facial expressions, and the same raising of his right hand in the Nazi salute.

Then the old man closed his eyes and abruptly fell asleep.

"His mind wanders sometimes," said Egon quietly. "Some days are better than others. He used to have a sharp wit, and he can still come up with a pithy reply, especially if you challenge him with a direct question. But if the conversation lags, he has four or five stories that he tells over and over again, although I don't think he's aware that he's repeating himself. We brought him over to the States to live with us when his memory started to go. I didn't want him to spend his last days with strangers in some kind of retirement home. He's been through a lot in his lifetime."

Margit was touched by Egon's obvious love for his father. It couldn't be easy for him to take care of the old man alone. She thought about Renny's aunt, whose failing mind was also making her lose her grip on the present. Renny once told Margit sadly, "Aunt Olive is just like that satellite that got loose from the space shuttle and sailed off into the darkness with its tether trailing behind. And there was no way to bring it back. The only thing the astronauts could do was watch helplessly as it drifted away into oblivion. One day Aunt Olive is going to be lost to us for good, too."

Margit shivered and decided to get back to the purpose of her visit. She picked up her coffee cup, took a sip, and said to Egon, "You were telling me how the situation in Denmark began to change in the summer of '43."

"Oh yes. Well, as I said, there were general strikes in August that were especially volatile in Jutland and on Fyn. Things had been getting worse all the time, and the mood among the people was shifting. By then everyone was used to shortages and rationing—no coffee or tea, no wheat after the bad harvest the year before. But tensions were rising, and the Germans were getting more hostile as the acts of sabotage against them were being stepped up. Then in late September, Hitler decided to round up the Danish Jews."

"I heard about that from my father," said Margit. "He told me that almost all the Jews were safely transported to Sweden."

"Yes, it was an amazing effort—truly heroic. In a matter of weeks more than 7,000 people were saved by sending them across Øresund to Sweden which, as you know, was neutral during the war. A huge underground rescue operation was quickly mobilized, and the S.I. took an active part in it. Lots of organizations got involved, and that's when people in the medical profession jumped in and played a leading role. Doctors and other hospital personnel already had a network of colleagues they could turn to for help. They tended to be people of high moral standards. And the hospitals were ideal places for temporarily hiding refugees until boats could be found to ferry them across to Sweden."

"Gudrun Madsen must have been a young medical student at the time," mused Margit, starting to wonder about a possible connection between her death and those events of long ago. "Toril told me the coin was popular among doctors, but she said it wasn't produced until 1944."

"Yes, well, after the push to rescue the Jews was over, people suddenly realized that Denmark was not completely cut off from the rest of the world after all. The waters between Denmark and Sweden were patrolled and mined. And the passage was always a dangerous one, even across the shortest distance between Helsingør and Hälsingborg. But several corridors had been opened up, and all of a sudden an extensive covert system was in place for transporting people and goods. There was a surge of illegal maritime traffic across Øresund during the last year and a half of the war. The doctors played a lesser role in this next stage of activity, but they were still staunch supporters of the resistance, and they bought a lot of those coins."

"The inscriptions on the coin seem to be warnings of some kind," said Margit, leaning forward, thoroughly gripped by what she was hearing.

Egon nodded and then said soberly, "Yes, they had to do with the policy of the *Nacht und Nebel Erlass*."

"What's that?"

"The Dead-of-Night Decree—an order secretly issued by Hitler back in '41, stating that action against the occupying power was punishable by death. If execution couldn't be carried out within a week after the suspect's arrest, or if the war court in the occupied country decided that it couldn't hand down the death penalty, then the prisoner was to be deported to Germany, 'in the dead of night.' There he would be 'isolated from the rest of the world,' as the decree so delicately put it." Egon shook his head.

"Anyway, Denmark was the one country excluded from this order, which applied to all other occupied territories. But that changed in the fall of '43. The Gestapo set up operations in Denmark, and suddenly informers were more dangerous than ever. People involved in any kind of resistance activities had to be extremely vigilant. If someone handed you one of those coins, you knew it meant trouble and you'd better watch your step."

Egon's expression turned grim. "We lost a lot of good people in the S.I. because of the traitors who fed information to the Germans."

"Why do you suppose a coin like this would show up at a murder scene here in Seattle?" asked Margit. "Do you think Dr. Madsen was involved in the Danish resistance? And if she was, do you think she might have actually been killed because of events that happened over fifty years ago?"

"I have no idea," said Egon. "But that was a terrible time in our history. There were many unheralded acts of bravery performed by ordinary citizens who refused to sit still in the face of evil. But there were also hidden acts of treachery committed by people who were driven by greed or a lust for power. I've met a few people like that in my day, and I know one thing for sure— if you cross them, they're not the kind who would ever forgive... or forget."

12

A cool breeze washed over Margit's face as she rolled the car window farther down, and then stomped on the accelerator to pass an old Pontiac clunker that was poking along in the left lane. It was Monday evening and she was heading east across the wide arch of the West Seattle bridge, glad she wasn't stuck in the bumper-to-bumper traffic inching its way along in the other direction. During the morning and evening rush hours, the six-lane stretch of freeway across the bridge was one of the busiest roads in the whole state. Thank God for telecommunications and the freelance life, thought Margit. She didn't want to commute to work ever again.

She was pleased to see clouds gathering overhead. It would be a relief to get some rain. The high temperatures and unbroken sunshine for the past few weeks were unnatural phenomena in Seattle, and everyone was beginning to wilt. Even the Fourth of July had been sunny—for the first time in eight years.

Margit glanced off to her right and noted that the top half of Mt. Rainier was cloaked in mist. With an elevation of over

14,000 feet, the mountain produced its own weather system. Clear skies in the entire Puget Sound area didn't guarantee a sunny day on the slopes, sixty miles to the southeast.

It was hard to believe that the familiar snow-covered landmark could easily turn deadly. Seattleites had witnessed the plume of the Mt. Saint Helens eruption from viewpoints all over the city. And Margit would never forget those eerie TV pictures of Yakima, when day suddenly became night and ash nearly buried the town. She could understand why scientists described the nightmare of a volcanic eruption as nothing short of "biblical." But it was still impossible for most people to imagine the violent forces smoldering inside the pristine presence of Mt. Rainier.

Bryan Adams was wailing away on the car tape deck, singing a tune from his album *Waking up the Neighbors*. It made Margit think about her own next-door neighbor, Mr. Nettlebury, who had been complaining lately about the bad drummer down the street.

"The guy is driving me crazy," he told Margit just the day before. "How am I supposed to get any shuteye with all that racket?" Mr. Nettlebury slept during the day because he worked the graveyard shift at a local convenience store. Every afternoon the drummer's practice session woke him up.

Margit had to agree that the guy was probably the world's worst musician, with absolutely no sense of rhythm or beat. Whenever he started up, she would grit her teeth and try desperately to find some coherent pattern to his playing. The suspense of waiting for the next drumbeat was like waiting for the other shoe to drop. Fortunately, the guy didn't have any staying power, and he rarely played more than half an hour.

Margit took the exit for the viaduct and merged into the

traffic moving north along 99. She was on her way to meet Detective Tristano at a restaurant over by Green Lake, but she wasn't sure why. Instead of calling, he had sent her a peremptory email message, which she found rather annoying.

"Need to talk. Meet at Lakeside Café, 75th and Greenwood. 6:00 tonight. Let me know if you can make it. A. Tristano."

Margit had kept her reply equally curt. "OK. I'll be there. M. Andersson."

After she sent the message, she regretted signing her name that way. But the detective's stubborn insistence on formality was starting to border on the absurd, and she couldn't resist giving him a little gibe about it. He probably wouldn't even notice.

Margit passed the Washington State ferry terminal and suddenly remembered another bright summer evening just about a year ago. It was exactly at this spot, as she and Joe were driving along the viaduct on their way to a party, that the forbidding shape of a B-2 stealth bomber passed close overhead. It looked like a huge flying wedge—painted a dull black and completely unreal. Margit felt as if she were in some kind of cartoon or a bad Ed Wood movie. In a few seconds it was gone, becoming a straight black line in the distance, on its approach to Boeing Field.

"My God, that was scary," Margit had whispered. But Joe didn't see anything apocalyptic about the plane; in fact, he gave her a long speech about the sculptural purity of the design. She should have realized then that they might not be suited to each other.

Margit sighed and pushed back her hair from her face. She had spent the whole day translating the Swedish medical job for Lars, too busy to think about anything else. It took her till five o'clock to finish, and then she had modemed it over to Liisa at the agency. Brian once asked her how she could stand to translate such tedious documents, but Margit told him that she actually preferred the dry, scientific language of doctors and engineers.

"You just have to learn the vocabulary specific to the topic, and then the translation is usually pretty straightforward," she explained. "And you don't have to wrestle with problems of interpretation the way you do with magazine or newspaper articles. They're a lot harder to translate because the writing can be so exaggerated and self-indulgent."

And the more repetition in a job, the better. It meant that she didn't have to spend time looking up as many terms, and she could even program entire phrases into "hot keys" on her computer instead of typing them out. Since technical translation was basically piecework—paid by the word, not by the hour—efficiency was just as essential as accuracy.

Margit drove along Phinney Ridge, past the big Starbucks coffee shop, wishing she had time to stop for an espresso, but she was already five minutes late. She passed an art gallery that she remembered visiting with Renny a few months back, but otherwise she wasn't very familiar with this part of the city. Margit slowed down, looking for the Lakeside Café.

At 75th and Greenwood she spotted the blue-and-white awning of Yanni's Greek Cuisine, but no Lakeside. There was a tavern on the other corner, a car repair shop across the street, and a few small businesses tucked into storefronts along the block. She went as far as 80th without finding the café. Then she turned around and slowly drove back, scanning the names of the stores again. But the Greek place was the only restaurant.

Great, thought Margit, feeling exasperated. Now what?

Then she caught sight of the detective waving to her from the restaurant window, so she parked the car and went in.

"Sorry about that," said Tristano, looking embarrassed as he pulled out a chair for Margit and then sat down across from her. "I haven't been here in a while. I didn't realize they'd changed the name."

"That's OK," said Margit, noting that her heart was beating too fast and her face felt flushed. Take it easy, she told herself. This isn't a date. At least she didn't think so, although she was pleased to see that the detective hadn't brought his partner along.

"I've got some more things I wanted to ask you regarding the Queen Anne murder," said Tristano briskly. "Thought I might as well buy you dinner for your trouble. Hope it wasn't too inconvenient coming to this part of town. I have to interview a witness over in Wallingford about another case around eight."

So this was official police business, after all, thought Margit, dismayed by the detective's guarded expression and stern tone of voice. But maybe he was like Brian and had trouble switching out of his professional role when he was in the middle of an investigation—even if he didn't have to wear a uniform. She decided to give him the benefit of the doubt and stop being so critical. She asked him with a smile, "Why Greek? I thought you would have preferred Italian food."

"No, my mother is such a great cook that Italian restaurants are usually a disappointment," he said, and some of the tension seemed to leave his face. "When I go out to eat, I like to try other ethnic foods—especially anything with a lot of garlic."

"That certainly lets out the Scandinavians, doesn't it?" said Margit with a laugh.

Tristano admitted that he had been surprised by the blandness of Danish cuisine during their trip to Copenhagen, although he had become a big fan of *stegt rødspætte*—flounder dipped in bread crumbs and sautéed in butter to a golden brown.

There was a moment of awkward silence. The detective stared out the window at a car racing past, clearly exceeding the speed limit. Margit took a sip of water and then glanced around the restaurant, feeling suddenly depressed. It was a cozy little place decorated with wine kegs, fake ivy, bunches of shimmering glass grapes, and neatly framed photographs of Mediterranean beaches. The lighting was appropriately dimmed for an intimate tête-à-tête. But Margit realized now that the possibilities sparked by that unexpected kiss back in Denmark had faded over the intervening months of non-communication.

"Maybe we'd better order," said Tristano abruptly, picking up the menu and perusing the list of entrees. Margit decided on vegetarian cabbage rolls with a Greek salad, and the detective chose chicken souvlaki with avgolemono soup. While they waited for the food, Tristano pulled out a small leather notebook from his briefcase and handed it to Margit.

"This was in the bottom drawer of Dr. Madsen's desk. Some of the notes are in Danish and we wondered if you could take a look and see if there's anything interesting."

Margit carefully read each Danish entry, but they were all completely mundane items, such as lists of groceries to buy, a recipe or two, and the titles of a few Danish books. Nothing seemed relevant to the investigation.

"We've been interviewing people who knew the doctor," said the detective. "By all accounts she led an extremely quiet life. She was well-liked and respected, but she didn't socialize much, especially after retiring from her medical practice. She was supposed to go to a barbecue on the Fourth of July hosted by old friends, but they said she called the day before and canceled.

"We know even less about Mrs. Nørgaard," Tristano added. "So far the Danish police haven't found any living relatives, and her neighbors had no idea why she would come to Seattle. They said that she seemed to be getting a little crazy lately." Then the detective took out a deckle-edged photograph and placed it on the table in front of Margit.

She picked up the black-and-white snapshot to examine it more closely. Two girls wearing old-fashioned bathing suits were sitting side by side on a rocky beach. They were smiling happily, and they had their faces lifted toward the sun. It didn't take Margit more than a moment to recognize Gudrun Madsen and Rosa Nørgaard, even though the picture must have been taken sometime back in the thirties.

"So they *were* friends," she said, looking up.

"Yes," said the detective. "We talked to Dr. Madsen's daughter, and she remembers her mother mentioning a childhood pen pal named Rosa who lived in Sweden. The name stuck in her mind because her mother rarely discussed the past. In fact, according to her daughter, Dr. Madsen seemed to take great pains to avoid talking about any part of her life before she got married and came to the States. We found the photograph in her night stand."

"Huh. Well, Rosa must have been visiting Denmark when this picture was taken," said Margit, handing it back to Tristano. "See the castle off in the distance? That's Kronborg, Hamlet's castle, in Helsingør."

Their dinners arrived just then, and as Margit picked up her fork, she added, "Did you know that Helsingør is only five kilometers away from the Swedish coast? I looked it up because I remembered reading in the paper that it was Dr. Madsen's home town. And I'm starting to wonder whether she might have been involved in some kind of illegal traffic across the water during the war."

Then Margit told Tristano everything that Egon Kirkeby had said about the copper coin and its connection to the medical profession and the Danish resistance movement.

"Apparently one of the regular ferry boats continued to operate between Helsingør and Hälsingborg during the war, but the route was also used by all the major organizations secretly transporting refugees and couriers across Øresund. Egon told me that his group, the S.I., was mainly interested in the transport of so-called 'heavy mail' in the opposite direction—taking weapons, ammunition, explosives, and radio equipment from Sweden to Denmark. And I guess they were quite successful at it."

"So you think that Dr. Madsen—and maybe even Mrs. Nørgaard—might have been mixed up in these activities?" asked the detective.

"Yes, I think it's possible. Egon said that the route network in the provincial ports was largely based on personal contacts, especially in the beginning. The groups had to find individuals they could trust to house the refugees before departure, to act as messengers, and to skipper the boats across Øresund. So people would naturally turn to their friends for help. Here were two girlfriends living on opposite sides of the water, and one of them had ties to a profession that was already active in the resistance. Seems like a perfect setup."

"But even if they were involved somehow, why would this have anything to do with Dr. Madsen's murder?"

"Well, I don't really know. But why was that coin found near her body? Why was Rosa Nørgaard coming to Seattle? And why did she suddenly die at the airport like that?"

Margit raised her hand to stop Tristano from protesting. "I

know it was a heart attack—but I was there and I heard what she said. And if Gudrun Madsen was at the airport to meet Rosa, why didn't she come forward when the police tried to find someone waiting for her? And don't you think it's a big coincidence that Dr. Madsen should end up murdered only a few hours later?" Margit could hear that her voice was getting shrill, but she was suddenly irritated by the detective's cautious skepticism when he didn't seem to have any better theory himself.

She finished her dinner and pushed the plate aside. Then she leaned her chin on her hand and said somberly, "Egon told me about another issue that people don't usually like to mention. He said that huge sums of money were spent to keep the routes in operation. There's no question that the men who sailed the boats back and forth across Øresund performed a heroic service at great personal risk. But most of them were well paid for it. During the effort to rescue the Jews, for example, the accepted price for transport was between 500 and 2,000 kroner per person. Egon said this didn't mean that people were left behind if they couldn't pay, because funds were set up to cover the passage for those who couldn't afford it. But there was clearly a lot of money to be made, and some people took in a handsome profit. And that kind of money always attracts a certain number of unscrupulous characters."

"But Mr. Kirkeby didn't know whether Dr. Madsen was actually working for the resistance or not?" asked the detective.

"No, he didn't. But he told me that at the height of all the activity, there were well over a thousand people involved with the Øresund routes. And because of the nature of the work, many people used pseudonyms instead of their real names."

A waiter came over to clear away the dinner plates. They both ordered coffee but declined dessert.

Then Margit leaned over the table and said, "Apparently not everybody worked with the established refugee and intelligence organizations, either. According to Egon, there were also quite a few freelancers."

13

Heavy clouds rolled in from the coast overnight, and the temperature dropped to a cool 62 degrees. Tuesday started out with gray skies and a light drizzle. At nine o'clock Margit left the house wearing jeans, running shoes, and an old Bumbershoot sweatshirt. She paused for a moment on the front walkway and smiled at the rain tickling her face. Even Gregor looked happy as he sniffed at the air and then jauntily flicked the tip of his tail before he set off for the communal cat track along the side of the house.

Margit drove over to the West Seattle post office to pick up her mail. I've been living here too long, she thought to herself with a laugh. I'm turning into a real Northwesterner—grumbling about sunshine and hot weather, and then cheering up when it starts to rain.

She pulled into one of the three parking slots in front of the post office, waiting for No Doubt to finish playing "Don't Speak" before she turned off the engine. What a great band, thought Margit as she got out of the car.

Lately she had started to wonder whether her taste in music might be getting a little stale—especially after Renny's niece took one look at her CD collection and pronounced it "so uncool that it's cool." Margit wasn't sure she liked being labeled "retro," so she decided to take the advice of an earnest young sales clerk at Silver Platters and try out some of the new groups. She would never lose her love for Motown or her admiration for the skillful musicianship of the bands from the seventies. But she had to admit that some of the newer groups were actually quite good. Their youthful energy was contagious, and their playing was getting more sophisticated. Margit was glad to hear that the incomprehensible ranting of Seattle's famous grunge sound was finally passé. Some of the groups were starting to sing understandable lyrics again, and their darkly comic view of life in the nineties appealed to her own sense of irony.

Margit pulled a handful of envelopes and a few magazines out of her post office box, relieved that she didn't have to deal with all the unwanted junk mail that used to be delivered to her house. She no longer got anything generically addressed to "Occupant." Before heading back to the car, she stood in the lobby and flipped through the assortment of bills and other mail. She stopped when she came to an official airline envelope with Brian's familiar, back-slanted handwriting on the front.

Hoping it was her paycheck, Margit used her car key to slit open the envelope. To her surprise, she found another letter inside, addressed to "Miss Andersen, Interpreter, c/o Star Air, Sea-Tac Airport." Brian had stuck a bright pink Post-It note on top and written: "This came in the mail Saturday. Don insists it's a love letter from an admirer. Maybe it will give you a laugh. See you Thursday."

But Margit wasn't laughing when she opened the envelope and read the one-line message typed on the enclosed card.

"Oh my God," she gasped. Then she ran out of the post office, yanked open the door to the Mazda, and jumped into the driver's seat. Tossing the rest of the mail onto the dashboard, she picked up the car phone and dialed the police.

Her call was transferred to Detective Silikov.

"Ms. Andersson? Nice to hear from you again. What can we do for you?"

"I just got a note from the murderer," said Margit, her voice quavering. "It was sent to the airport last Saturday, and my friend had it forwarded to me."

"Why do you think it's from the murderer?" asked the detective. "What does it say?"

Margit took a deep breath, feeling sick to her stomach. She looked down at the card in her hand. "It says the same thing as the coin. It says, '*Gaa stille med dørene.*'"

There was a brief silence on the line and then Silikov asked sharply, "Anything else? Is it signed?"

"No," said Margit. "That's all. But my last name is misspelled on the envelope—it's spelled the Danish way, with an '-*sen*' instead of '-*sson*.' And the card has a photo on the front. It's a picture of a raven." She didn't think she needed to explain to the detective the ominous significance of that choice of image.

"OK, here's what I want you to do. Put the card back in the envelope and then stick it inside another envelope or in a paper bag. Not plastic—we don't want any moisture to get sealed up inside. Maybe we'll be able to get some prints off the card. I'm tied up with something else right now, but I'm going over to the memorial service for Dr. Madsen at one o'clock. I can swing by your place afterwards and pick up the card."

"Where's the service going to be held?" asked Margit. "I could meet you there." She had a sudden impulse to pay her respects to the dead woman, even though they had never met. Chance had inextricably drawn her into the lives of Gudrun Madsen and Rosa Nørgaard. The shock of witnessing the old woman's death at the airport had been compounded by the murder of the doctor. When Tristano showed Margit the photograph of the two girls happily posing on the Danish beach, she suddenly found herself looking at the beginning of a story to which she already knew the end. For some reason she felt an urgent need to find out what had happened in between. What had become of the innocence and promise of those two young lives? And why did those two women, so many years later, have to die the way they did?

Margit looked down at the picture of the raven on the card she was holding. The threat scared her but it also made her stubborn. She tightened her grip on the car phone. "I really would like to attend the memorial service," she told Silikov again. "I'll bring the card with me."

So the detective gave Margit the address of a funeral chapel in Lower Queen Anne, which she scribbled on the back of an old BP receipt she found in the glove compartment. Then she said goodbye and put down the phone. With trembling fingers she slid the card first into its own envelope and then inside the airline envelope that Brian had used. Next, she placed it carefully on the passenger seat beside her and piled the rest of the mail on top. She knew this was a childish gesture, but the card was giving her the jitters and she didn't want to look at it anymore.

For a moment Margit sat motionless, staring at the rain trickling down the windshield. All trace of her earlier exuberance at the change in the weather was now gone.

She was thinking back to last Thursday when the station manager had called her into his office to tease her about a man asking questions at the gate. What was it Don had said?

"This guy came up and asked me your name and all kinds of questions about you... Could have been your father. Had some weird accent too."

Whoever had sent this card knew that she worked at the airport, knew that she had been present when Rosa Nørgaard died, and knew about the connection between Rosa and Dr. Madsen. And he also knew about the copper coin before the police told anyone else about it, since the card must have been mailed on Friday.

Margit shuddered and then glanced up and caught sight of her anxious face in the rearview mirror. She was suddenly reminded of her mother's penchant for quoting Danish proverbs at appropriate moments. When Margit was a kid and things seemed to be going all wrong, her mother would pat her hand sympathetically and say: "*Ingenting er så galt, at det ikke er godt for noget*"—nothing is so bad that it isn't good for something.

Margit shook back her hair and smiled. OK, cheer up, she told herself. Listen to your mother.

Then she started up the engine, turned on the windshield wipers, and swiftly pulled out of the parking lot onto California Avenue.

She spent the next two hours ironing several loads of laundry in the bedroom while she listened to the Neville Brothers, turned up full blast. Margit always ironed when she needed some

distraction to calm herself down. It was a soothing and me-
thodical activity. She ironed practically everything, even her un-
derwear and t-shirts, folding them up and stacking them on the
bed. Gregor always kept her company, sitting as close to the
freshly ironed shirts as he could get. He seemed to have a real
fetish for clean laundry; Margit would sometimes find him asleep
in the wicker laundry basket, burrowed under a layer of newly
washed sheets or towels.

The phone rang as she was putting away the ironing board.
Margit glanced at the alarm clock on the nightstand to check on
the time before she ran down the hall to her study. It was 11:30,
so she only had an hour before she had to leave for the memorial service. If Liisa was calling about another rush translation
job that had to be done by the end of the day, she would just
have to find someone else to handle it.

But it wasn't Liisa on the line. It was Margit's father.

"*Hej Pappa, hur mår du?*" said Margit, dropping into a chair
and propping her legs up on her desk.

Her father occasionally called her at odd hours of the day,
just to chat. Carl Andersson had taught philosophy and medi-
eval history at a private high school in St. Paul, but a year ago
he had retired. At his retirement party, he announced to everyone that finally he was going to write those books he had been
thinking about for years—but so far he hadn't made much
progress. He was still a little unnerved by all the free time suddenly at his disposal after giving up his busy teaching schedule.
And Carl admitted that he hadn't reckoned with the feelings of
depression and lassitude that overwhelmed him once in a while.
Margit figured that her father was simply feeling a little lonely,
since he no longer had colleagues or students to talk to on a
daily basis. And her mother, Janna, wasn't home during the day

because she worked full-time as a librarian at the University of Minnesota.

Margit chatted with her father about the weather and the latest political scandals, and then she found herself telling him all about the murder investigation.

When she came to the part about the S.I. and the traffic across Øresund during the war, Carl suddenly interrupted her.

"My uncle worked for the Danish-Swedish Refugee Service in '44 and '45, you know."

"You're kidding. You never told me that before," said Margit in surprise.

"Didn't I? Well, maybe I thought you wouldn't be interested."

Margit winced at this remark, remembering a few impertinent speeches she had made as a teenager, chastising her father for what she called "your generation's fixation on World War II." Her own childhood had been marked by the social and political upheaval of the sixties, and she had watched the Vietnam war take the lives of boys only a few years older than herself. But even so, Margit had to admit that she and many of her peers largely failed to comprehend the catastrophic effect that the last Great War must have had on their parents and grandparents. And she realized that as subsequent generations became absorbed in the throes of their own lives, they would find it even harder to see what relevance a rehashing of those past events could possibly have for them.

"I'm sorry if I gave you that impression," Margit told her father. "Of course I'm interested. Did your uncle work with the Øresund routes?"

"Yes, he did. I was only twelve back then, but I remember that he spent a lot of time in Malmö and Hälsingborg. He never talked about his work whenever he came home to visit his family in Uppsala. But after the war was over, he told me stories about the ships sailing back and forth across Øresund. In fact, you were named for one of them."

"What?" exclaimed Margit. "What do you mean? I thought I was named for Tove Ditlevsen. Wasn't Margit one of her middle names?"

"Yes—and that's what your mother thinks too. When you were born and I suggested that we call you 'Margit,' Janna agreed at once because she liked the idea of naming you after a famous author. I decided not to tell her where I actually got the name from, since she had such bad memories about the war."

"So where *did* you get the name from?" asked Margit, astonished by this news. But she was reminded again that her mother had always been a little reticent about those years of her childhood, although Janna did admit to certain habits that could be attributed to the shortages she experienced as a kid. She kept large quantities of canned goods in the basement, "in case of emergency," as she always said. She also hoarded bars of expensive perfumed soap. Janna was only six when the occupation started, but she vividly remembered the rough soap mixed with clay that was soon the only kind available in Denmark. And Margit recalled that when the blast of the factory whistles still signaled the noon hour in St. Paul, her mother sometimes used to say that they reminded her of air-raid sirens.

Margit swung her legs down from her desk and sat up straight, trying to focus on what her father was saying on the phone.

Carl was talking about his uncle again. "He told me that in February of '44 the Refugee Service added another ship to its fleet of vessels—a sleek cutter that was almost ten meters long. The boat was purchased from a well-to-do merchant in

Havstenssund for 12,000 Swedish kronor, which was apparently peanuts for such a good sailing ship. It was registered as SD-712, and it was named the *Margit*.

"My uncle showed me a picture of it," continued Carl. "A beautiful boat, and it made a big impression on me. It once carried thirty-nine passengers in a single crossing."

"So it was mainly used for transporting refugees?" asked Margit, still stunned by this revelation of her namesake.

"Refugees and contraband. When it got too dangerous for ships to sail all the way across Øresund, a system was developed called 'kontaktsejling.' This meant that two ships would depart from opposite shores and make contact at some prearranged spot to exchange cargo. A couple of times a week, the *Margit* would sail from Hälsingborg out to the lightship at Lappegrund and rendezvous with a Danish boat."

"Why didn't the Germans put a stop to all this traffic between Denmark and Sweden?"

"Well, it was a long coastline to patrol, and the Germans already had their hands full trying to counter the sharp rise in sabotage and other illegal activities going on all over Denmark. But plenty of people involved in the route networks did get caught, and it was always a very risky business. My uncle told me that the head of the biggest group in Helsingør was arrested in the spring of '44 and sent to Vestre Prison and then deported to Germany. Informers were always the worst problem. One night in Gilleleje, someone betrayed a pastor and the 120 refugees he had hidden in his church, and they were all rounded up by the Germans. Route workers who were identified were often targeted for 'liquidation'—murdered in their beds or shot down in cold blood in the middle of the street."

Carl paused for a moment and then went on. "I was only a

boy at the time, and I spent the war years living safely in neutral Sweden, so I thought all of my uncle's stories were pretty exciting. But looking back as an adult, I realize it was a terrible time. The level of tension and suspicion must have been enormous. And as the route networks grew, it evidently got harder to know who to trust. I guess the personal conflicts didn't make things any easier, either."

"What do you mean?" asked Margit.

"My uncle said that the people who worked with the Øresund routes were notoriously independent. They were mostly well educated, self-reliant, and used to exercising authority. This meant that they were good at finding ingenious ways to transport people and cargo. But it also meant that clashes were common, both between organizations and within individual groups. There were fights over proprietary rights to certain rendezvous points for the boats. There was competition for the services of expert skippers. And, of course, there were always conflicts about money."

"Egon Kirkeby told me that huge sums were involved in the Øresund traffic," said Margit.

"Yes, that's what my uncle said too. It took a lot of cash to hire or buy boats and to keep them all running—plus the people operating them had to be paid. And sometimes there were problems: the occasional dishonest skipper who simply absconded with the advance payment, or others who jacked up the price halfway across. And the boats also carried large amounts of cash as part of their cargo. People often had to flee quickly, with only the clothes on their backs; but once they arrived in Sweden, they would send for whatever savings they had left behind. The refugee organizations agreed to transport these funds for a standard payment of 10%."

"I wonder whether a few people might have been tempted to take a bigger percentage," mused Margit.

"I don't know," said her father. "But I suppose it's possible. You know what your mother always says: '*Penge makker mod, og armod makker kunster.*'"

Margit was still thinking about that proverb as she hung up the phone a few minutes later. "Money bolsters courage, and poverty bolsters cunning."

14

Margit arrived at the memorial service for Gudrun Madsen about ten minutes late. Everyone else had already taken their places inside, and muted organ music was drifting out of the open doorway. The foyer was deserted except for a doleful-looking man wearing a dark suit who apparently worked for the funeral chapel.

He came forward, murmured a few pat phrases of condolence, and then handed Margit a program printed on rose-colored paper. On the front was the same photo of Dr. Madsen that had been used in the newspapers—the one in which she was wearing the necklace with the Thor's hammer. Inside the program there was a hymn by Thomas Kingo in both Danish and English, along with a list of those who were going to participate in the service. Margit stopped to sign the guest book and then stepped inside the dimly lit chapel and sat down in the last pew, to the right of the doorway.

As she peered at the assembled mourners, she thought about the signature that had caught her eye at the top of the page in the guest book. Someone had written in a bold, flowing script: "Göran Hultén." Now where had she seen that name before? It looked familiar, but she just couldn't place it.

When Margit's eyes adjusted to the shadowy light, she saw that Detective Silikov was seated against the wall, on the opposite side of the aisle, three rows ahead of her. Toril Christensen was sitting in front, and there were close to a hundred other people in attendance. At least half of the guests appeared to be in their thirties and forties — many of them must have been Dr. Madsen's patients when they were kids.

A thin elderly woman wearing a plain brown dress stepped up to the lectern and squinted at the harsh spotlight. She paused for a moment to adjust her reading glasses and to smooth out the sheet of paper that she had placed in front of her. Then she began speaking with a distinct Swedish accent.

Margit stared at the lovely arrangements of roses and lilies gracing the front of the chapel as she listened to the words of praise for Gudrun Madsen. The doctor was described as a kind and compassionate person who had a special affinity with children, which had obviously led to her choice of profession. For years she had been much in demand as the pediatrician for so many families in Seattle's Scandinavian community. The speaker began to tell anecdotes about various people — now grown-up and respected citizens themselves — whose broken arms, gashed knees, and cases of chicken pox had been treated by the doctor.

A few minutes later Margit decided to slip away and wait for the detective outside. It was obvious that she wasn't going to learn any more about Gudrun Madsen's early life, and the mood of tight restraint among the guests was getting hard to take. Several people were nervously rustling the programs they were holding, and a woman across the aisle sniffed a couple of times and then pulled a handkerchief out of her purse to dab at her eyes. But most people were sitting in rigid silence and staring straight ahead.

It seemed clear from both the eulogy and the size of the crowd that the demise of the doctor was truly mourned, but no one felt free to weep openly. Their Scandinavian upbringing had instilled in them a strict prohibition against public displays of emotion. And yet the tension created by holding their grief inside was more excruciating than any loud cries of lament would have been.

Margit was well aware that this inculcated reserve was part of her own personality. She found it a useful trait in dealing with overly nosy or pushy types of people, especially in work situations. But she also recognized that it fostered a certain coldness of spirit, which she found disturbing. For years she had been trying to find ways to overcome this tendency to suppress her real feelings. She once told Renny that she wished she could allow herself five minutes each morning to sit down and have a good cry, the way Holly Hunter did in the movie *Broadcast News.*

As the next speaker approached the lectern to pay tribute to the deceased, Margit unobtrusively left the funeral chapel and stepped outside the building. The rain had stopped and the sun was trying valiantly to break through the clouds. Margit figured that it would probably be another half hour before the service ended and she could hand over the raven card to Detective Silikov.

She glanced up and noticed the Space Needle looming like a beacon above the Seattle Center, which had served as the site of the World's Fair back in 1962. The area had since been turned into the city's largest arts and entertainment venue, boasting several theaters and sports arenas. The spacious grounds were only a few blocks away, so Margit decided to go over and take a walk around.

On her way to the Center she passed a bookstore, which reminded her of what Tristano had told her as they finished their coffee in the Greek restaurant the night before.

"We've been working on what it said in the letter that you translated for us—the one we lifted from the impressions on Dr. Madsen's notepad. As you may recall, it said: 'I'll wait for you at the bookstore.' We've gone to nearly every bookstore in town, trying to find out whether anyone remembered seeing the doctor recently. This afternoon all our legwork finally paid off."

"Someone saw her?" asked Margit.

"Yes, one of the employees in the café at the Elliott Bay Book Company. He hadn't read the news about the murder, but he recognized Dr. Madsen from the photo we showed him. He said he remembered her because he had just started his shift, and she ordered a glass of red wine, which he thought was an odd choice for ten o'clock in the morning. He said she seemed worried and nervous, and she ended up spilling the wine all over the counter."

"That guy certainly has a good memory," said Margit. "I'm surprised he would remember a specific customer out of the hundreds he must see every week."

"Apparently it was the employee's birthday, and that's why he remembered the incident so well," said Tristano. "He told us that some of the red wine spattered onto the brand-new shirt he was wearing. It was a gift from his girlfriend, so he was a little ticked off."

"When did this happen?"

"It was last Thursday morning, July 10th."

"Two hours before Rosa arrived at the airport," said Margit. "Did the bookstore employee notice whether anyone was with Dr. Madsen?"

"He thought she was alone, but he had a vague recollection of seeing her leave in the company of a man. That might be the mysterious 'Muninn' that the letter was addressed to. Unfortunately, the employee couldn't give us any kind of description."

"What about the other line in the letter?" asked Margit. "Didn't it say something about 'catching the 9:25'?"

"Yes. We think that might refer to a ferry departure, since the proximity of the bookstore to the Colman Dock would make it a good place to meet. There's a 9:25 from Bainbridge Island, and the crossing only takes thirty-five minutes, so the timing would be right."

"What about the ferry from Bremerton?"

"No, that one leaves at 9:15. There are two other scheduled ferry departures at 9:25 on a weekday, but neither one arrives downtown. The Kingston ferry takes the same amount of time, but it docks up north in Edmonds, and that would involve an additional forty-minute drive at that time of day. The crossing from Vashon to West Seattle only takes fifteen minutes, but then it's at least a half-hour drive to downtown—and why would someone want to backtrack to meet at the bookstore if they were already halfway to the airport?"

"There's one other option," said Margit.

"What's that?"

"The passenger-only ferry from Vashon. I know there's a 9:25 departure because I've taken it a few times myself when I was housesitting for friends on the island. The boat docks downtown at the state ferry terminal, and it's an easy walk from there to the bookstore."

"I'd forgotten about that one," said Tristano, sounding surprised. "You could be right."

And that's where the conversation had ended because the detective had to rush off for his eight o'clock appointment. There was no time left for any personal remarks either, and Margit had driven home from the restaurant feeling a little disappointed.

What a chicken you are, she scolded herself now as she walked through the Seattle Center. Why didn't you say something? Why didn't you apologize for not returning his call after the Copenhagen trip? Then she sighed and glanced at her watch. Five more minutes and she'd have to go back.

Margit approached the rim of the International Fountain, dropped her shoulder bag onto a bench, and stood looking down at the sloping concrete sides of the enormous bowl-like structure. Rising up from the center of the fountain was a huge silver dome that reminded Margit of a comic-book drawing of a flying saucer. Great sprays of water were shooting out of the embedded nozzles in an alternating pattern, rising more than thirty feet into the air.

She wondered whether the man asking questions about her at the airport was the same man who had met Gudrun Madsen at the bookstore. She wondered whether he was the one who had pushed the doctor to her death late Thursday night—and then mailed the threatening card sometime on Friday.

Margit suddenly realized that she hadn't looked at the postmark. She opened her bag and pulled out the airline envelope, which still held the card. She didn't want to add any more of her own fingerprints to the evidence, so she carefully shook out the inner envelope just far enough to see the postmark. It was smudged and she couldn't read the zip code or the date, but it was possible to make out a blurry "VAS-."

There was no doubt that the card had been sent from Vashon Island.

At that moment a huge burst of water shot out of the fountain with an enormous whooshing sound, just like the spume of a whale. Margit jumped back with a startled shriek.

A young mother pushing a stroller along the nearby path stopped and asked with concern, "Are you all right?"

"I'm fine. Really—I'm fine. But thanks for asking," said Margit, feeling a little foolish. Then she stuck the card back in her bag, turned on her heel, and walked briskly through the grounds of the Seattle Center.

She reached the funeral chapel just as the last guests were leaving. Detective Silikov was standing on the sidewalk, talking intently to a woman with short silvery hair who wore a tailored black suit and flat, sensible shoes. Margit noticed at once that she bore a striking resemblance to Gudrun Madsen.

Must be the daughter from Montana, she thought, stopping a discreet distance away so as not to intrude on their conversation.

A few minutes later the detective helped the woman into a black sedan that was waiting at the curb. He shut the door gently and then watched the car slowly drive off.

"Was that Dr. Madsen's daughter?" asked Margit as she stepped up beside Detective Silikov.

"Oh, Ms. Andersson—there you are," he said, turning to give Margit a smile. "Yes, that was her daughter, Mrs. Bodil Woods. She wanted to know how the investigation was coming along."

As he spoke, the detective pulled out a gold pen and a small notebook from his pocket and carefully wrote something down.

Since she was standing right next to him, Margit couldn't help noticing what it said.

"*Moon Tiger*," she read aloud. "That's the title of a book."

"Yes, it is. Mrs. Woods happened to remember the name of the book this morning when she was thinking about the phone conversation she had with her mother last Wednesday. We asked her to try to reconstruct everything they talked about, because we never know what might prove relevant."

"Did Dr. Madsen mention anything about Rosa Nørgaard coming to visit?"

"No, she didn't. Mrs. Woods had no idea that her mother was even in contact with her childhood pen pal. She said Dr. Madsen seemed a little distracted, but otherwise perfectly normal. They discussed various family matters, and then her mother starting talking about this novel that she had been reading lately. She was evidently a great reader, and she was always recommending books for her daughter to buy. Mrs. Woods said that she seemed particularly taken with this one."

Detective Silikov put his notebook away and shrugged. "We'll have another look at the doctor's book collection and see if we can find a copy—just to make sure she didn't leave any secret messages in the margins. It's a long shot, but we have to follow up on anything that might be a lead."

"I know that book," said Margit. "It's an amazing novel by Penelope Lively. We read it in my book club just a few months ago. Do you know what it's about?"

The detective shook his head.

"Well, it's about an old woman who's on her deathbed and she decides to write the history of the world. But what she really ends up writing is her own history, as she thinks back on the events of her past and the time she spent in Egypt during the forties."

"I see," said the detective, but he didn't look particularly interested. Margit suspected that he wasn't much of a novel-reader himself. The outlandish real-life stories that a homicide detective uncovered on the job were probably enough to spoil anyone's taste for fiction.

"Now what about that card?" he asked.

So Margit gave the airline envelope and its contents to Detective Silikov. She also told him about the postmark, which indicated that the card had been mailed from Vashon.

Walking back to her car, Margit breathed a sigh of relief, glad that the evidence was now in the hands of the police. As she drove toward the viaduct entrance, she listened to Don Henley singing "Not Enough Love in the World." And she thought about the fact that she didn't get a chance to tell the detective something else about the book that Gudrun Madsen was reading. She didn't tell him that the real heart of the story was the old woman's memory of a brief but fateful love affair that she had had during the war.

15

Gregor emerged from his favorite spot under the spruce tree in the back yard when he heard the Mazda pull into the driveway. He strolled over to the car, rubbed his cheek against the bumper, and sniffed at the tires. Then he trotted up the path ahead of Margit and waited impatiently on the porch for her to open the front door.

"It's a cat's life," Margit told Gregor as she dropped her keys on the coffee table and slipped off her shoes. Then she sank onto the sofa and leaned wearily against the cushions. Gregor headed for the kitchen to have a snack, and Margit could hear him crunching on the dry food in his dish. He also had a peculiar habit of grumbling while he ate.

What a noisy eater, thought Margit affectionately as she closed her eyes and began to doze off.

A few minutes later Gregor was back, giving her a start as he jumped up onto her lap. In true cat fashion, he circled around twice before settling down with his head on her knee. Then he purred loudly as Margit stroked his shiny black fur.

She smiled and said, "You sure have it rough, don't you? You get to snooze all day long, you don't have to worry about house payments, and you never have to leave the neighborhood. Now if you could only learn to use a can opener, things would be perfect."

Just then the phone rang, and Margit managed to reach over and pick up the receiver from the end table without disturbing Gregor.

"Hi, kiddo," she heard Renny say cheerfully. "Where have you been all afternoon? I thought you were going to help me take my paintings over to the gallery."

"Oh no—was that today? Geez, I'm sorry, Renny. I forgot all about it," said Margit. "You wouldn't believe what I've been through."

Then she told her friend all about the raven card, the surprising phone conversation with her father, and the memorial service for the murdered doctor.

"And I thought *I* was having a bad day," said Renny. "Now promise me again that you won't do anything crazy—like trying to snoop around on your own."

"Don't worry. This whole investigation is getting way too complicated, and finding that card in my mailbox really gave me the creeps. I can just see myself having nightmares about it. Thank God my address isn't in the phone book, or I'd really be nervous. At least the guy doesn't know where I live."

But Margit felt a twinge of anxiety about those calls she had been getting recently with no one on the line. Maybe she ought to mention them to Tristano, although she couldn't see what good it would do.

"I hope the police can figure out what's going on," she told Renny. "And I hope they do it soon."

Margit leaned over to switch on the small table lamp, suddenly aware of how dark it was in the room. It was only four o'clock, but the skies had clouded up again and more rain seemed imminent.

"How'd it go at the gallery?" Margit asked Renny.

"OK, I guess. But I'm still not sure I really belong in that show." Renny had been invited to participate in a group exhibition of work by ten prominent African American painters. She was pleased to be included in such prestigious company, but she felt obliged to explain to the curator that her work was not necessarily race-oriented.

After her first meeting with the man (who happened to be white), Renny confided to Margit, "I told him that I paint what I paint, and I can't promise that my work will fit in with any specific theme or message. I also told him that my art has nothing to do with the diaspora. But I'm not sure he really believed me."

Margit knew that Renny was more interested in metaphysical than political issues, and that she hated being pigeonholed as a "woman painter" or a "black painter." She certainly didn't want to be expected to represent an entire gender or race. She once told Margit that the only label she was willing to accept was "twentieth-century American painter." Period. Although of course she also hoped to be considered a *good* painter.

"So which pieces did you and the curator finally agree on?"

"The three nudes that I finished last month and the painting of my Aunt Olive," said Renny.

That painting had made a strong impression on Margit. It was a large canvas showing a vast, dim landscape shadowed by heavy, low-lying clouds. The focal point of the work was the small, dark figure of a woman walking away from the viewer, about to be swallowed up by the encroaching dusk. Her body was overwhelmed by the sheer expanse of the surrounding plain, but strangely enough she was not a defeated figure. There was a certain dignity about her solitary retreat—a certain courage.

Renny had told Margit that the image for the painting came to her one day when she realized that the disintegrating effect of Alzheimer's was forcing her aunt to sever ties with everything familiar and set off alone into territory where no one else could follow. She had lost her grounding in the present, she had been stripped of any future, and now she was slipping farther and farther into the past. Soon even her most distant memories would be erased. To those left behind, she seemed to be moving uncontrollably toward a terrifying void, an absence of everything that had shaped her life and her person. To her family, it looked like a living death.

But Renny told Margit that she wanted to believe that her aunt's soul would be able to escape intact from the confusion of her deteriorating mind. And so she had titled the painting "A Plea for Her Spirit."

"You're not thinking of selling that painting, are you?" Margit asked Renny on the phone.

"Oh, no. That one's not for sale."

Then they talked about the opening of the show, which was planned for Saturday night, and a few minutes later Margit hung up.

As she sat on the sofa, petting Gregor, she remembered a passage from her childhood mythology book about the two ravens, Huginn and Muninn. Every morning Odin would send them out into the world to gather news for him. And each time the god let them go, he would worry that Huginn (or Thought) might not come back. But he dreaded even more the possibility that Muninn (or Memory) might fail to return.

This made Margit think about the way memory was constantly shaping a person's life. It was actually a reciprocal process, since each day everyone created new memories when sights, sounds, and smells were recorded and then stored away by the brain. Some of these accrued experiences would be pondered over and over; some would never be recalled again. But others might be evoked later, at an unexpected moment—involuntarily conjured up by a sudden flash of light, an odd smell, or a particular turn of phrase.

Margit thought about Egon Kirkeby's father and his memory of the Danish king, obviously prompted by overhearing words about the war. Proust was right when he showed that even something as inconsequential as a small delicate pastry could trigger vivid memories and summon up entire conversations that had seemed lost for good.

A few months back, Margit had translated several lengthy articles on the medical aspects of amnesia; at the time she had tried to imagine how devastating it must be for a person to lose both her identity and her past. But now she recalled an even stranger case she had heard about on TV. It was the story of a twenty-four-year-old man whose short-term memory had been destroyed by an aneurysm in his brain. He knew who he was, and he could remember people and events from before his illness—but he could no longer remember what he had eaten for lunch or who he had talked to during the day. Margit thought the most shocking thing about his condition was that he was incapable of assimilating any new memories.

This meant that his past had become fixed in time, and his

psyche was frozen forever in a twenty-four-year-old mind. The man would never really be thirty or forty or fifty because he couldn't process and store the experiences of his daily life as his body grew older. He couldn't learn and he couldn't change. He had a history but no future, since he couldn't acquire new memories to shape his thoughts or his outlook. And because of this, he was as cut off from normal human interaction as Renny's Aunt Olive was.

I wouldn't wish either condition on my worst enemy, thought Margit, shaking her head. Loss of memory was a terrible thing— although she could think of quite a few embarrassing episodes in her own past that she would just as soon forget. And some people, including her mother, probably wished they had more control over what they remembered, since unpleasant childhood memories continued to haunt them.

"Speaking of memory…" Margit said aloud, making Gregor open his eyes and twitch his ears. She suddenly wondered whether Don Schmidt could remember anything else about that man asking questions at the airport.

She picked up the phone again and dialed the Star Air number, but the station manager had already left for the day, and Brian wasn't in the office either.

"He went to Portland," said the airline agent who took the call. "One of our planes had to make an emergency landing, and since we don't have any regular staff there, Brian went down to take care of things. But he should be back by tomorrow."

"OK, thanks. I'll try him then," said Margit, hoping that Brian wasn't stuck with the same kind of passenger service nightmare that he had faced in Spokane only a few years ago. On that occasion, he had single-handedly dealt with the irate demands of several hundred stranded passengers. He told Margit that at one point he felt certain that he would either be trampled or lynched by the crowd.

But the ordeal he went through before even reaching the Spokane airport was worse.

Brian had told Margit all about that blustery February night when a Star Air 747 coming from Germany had been forced to make an emergency landing in Spokane. Warning lights indicated there was a fire on board, although it turned out to be a false alarm. But by then the extinguishers in the cargo hold had been activated, and the plane couldn't continue until they had been replaced. Since the only available replacements were back in Seattle, the Star Air chief engineer at Sea-Tac decided to hire a small plane to transport them to Spokane himself.

Brian went along to handle the three hundred anxious passengers who would have to be put up in hotels overnight, since there were no other flights to bring them to Seattle.

He told Margit that he was a little nervous when he saw the tiny four-seater Cessna and the two young pilots who were supposed to take them to Spokane. But he didn't really start to sweat until they were halfway across the mountains and the snowstorm set in. Visibility dropped to almost nil, and the winds began wildly buffeting the plane around. That's when he noticed that the Star Air engineer sitting next to him was shaking his head and muttering to himself.

Brian told Margit that he suddenly had a bad feeling in the pit of his stomach, but it wasn't due to airsickness. Something was wrong. He hesitated a few more minutes and then leaned over and shouted to be heard above the noise of the storm and the props, "What is it? What's going on?"

The engineer gave him a gloomy look and then shouted back, "If it gets much rougher, those things are going to blow up."

And he indicated with a backward jerk of his thumb the pressurized metal containers which held the fire-retardant chemicals.

"Are you serious?" yelled Brian.

"Yeah," shouted the engineer, his face grim. "Yeah, I'm serious all right."

The protective packing crates that normally housed the containers until they were installed had been left back in Seattle because they were too big to fit in the Cessna. And the only place to store the exposed containers on board was right behind the passenger seats.

When Brian looked at the engineer's worried expression, he realized that they were literally sitting on a bomb.

The last hour of the flight was tense.

He later told Margit that when they finally landed safely in snowy Spokane and the tiny plane taxied under the nose of the 747, he made a vow never to take that kind of risk again. It just wasn't worth it. For the first time he had envisioned his own death, and he pictured his wife and kids all alone. He might lose his job by refusing to take some future airline assignment—but at least he wouldn't lose his life.

Good thing it's summer now, thought Margit. A little rain was no big deal, and Brian wouldn't have to fly across the Cascades or any other mountain range to get to Portland.

"Just be glad *you* don't have to go out and earn a living," she told Gregor as she pushed him gently off her lap and stood up.

Thinking about Brian made Margit realize that she was a little uneasy about going back to the airport to fulfill her interpreting duties. After all, it was the one place where the murderer knew he could find her. And maybe he thought that Rosa

Nørgaard told her more than she did as she lay dying in the Immigration area at the airport. Margit wondered whether Rosa was thinking about the man named "Muninn" when she uttered those portentous words: "Not him!"

But Margit wasn't due back at Sea-Tac until Thursday, and she could always hope that the police would make a breakthrough in the case before then. In the meantime, she wasn't going to interfere with the investigation, but she might just do a little research on her own—that was one thing she was good at. And maybe she would find out something useful. Or maybe Renny was right, and she was just looking for another excuse to call up Detective Tristano. At any rate, she had the whole evening to herself since Liisa hadn't sent over any more rush translation jobs.

"Come on, Gregor, let's go down to the library," Margit said resolutely as she pulled her hair back into a ponytail and twisted a bright fuchsia elastic around her blonde tresses.

Gregor eagerly followed at her heels as she walked through the kitchen and opened the door to the basement stairs. When Margit moved into the house, she had hired a carpenter to build row upon row of shelves in the large basement, so that she could finally take her extensive book collection out of storage.

Renny said that the first time she stepped into Margit's basement, she felt herself transported back to the stacks of her neighborhood library, which she had visited every Friday night when she was a kid. She even caught herself looking around for the stern librarian who was always shushing any child who made too much noise.

Margit switched on the library lights at the bottom of the stairs and then slowly walked down one aisle, scanning the shelves on both sides. She had given away all her Old Norse texts after she finished grad school, but she seemed to remember seeing a volume on Nordic mythology among her history books.

If Gudrun Madsen had chosen Huginn for her code name during the war as Margit suspected, then it might be interesting to find out a few more details about Thor, Odin, and those two roaming ravens.

16

She is riding around in the back of an old truck in a bombed-out city. All of the buildings have been smashed to ruins. Jagged walls, teetering piles of dust-covered brick, broken glass, and great heaps of dirt are everywhere. There is an eerie silence. The only sound is the crunching of the truck tires on the rubble-filled road, the creaking of the vehicle's ancient springs, and the faint whispering of the two faceless people sitting up front. There is no other sound. Everyone else has left this mangled and desolate place. Everyone else has either fled or died. There is no sign of life and not a scrap of color. Everything is gray. Even the sky is a listless, gun-metal gray. She is riding around in the back of a decrepit truck, staring at the vicious wreckage of a dead city.

BANG!

Slam, BANG! Slam, BANG!

Bang-bang-bang-bang!

Slam, BAM!

Margit screamed as she lurched into a sitting position. Her heart was thundering, her pulse was racing, and sweat was pouring down her face. She peered into the shadows and finally recognized her bedroom bookcase, dresser, and chair. It was a shock and a relief to find herself in her own bed. Trembling, she reached over to snap on the reading light and then sank back against her pillows.

"My God," she whispered. "It's that damn drummer down the street." She glanced at the alarm clock on the nightstand. It was barely five in the morning, but the guy was madly flailing away on his drum kit. Had he suddenly become an early riser? Or was he suffering from a bout of insomnia? Did he decide that if *he* couldn't sleep, no one else in the neighborhood should either? Or was he totally oblivious to the penetrating range of the noise he was making? Could he possibly think that no one would hear him beyond the walls of his own house?

Margit stared up at the ceiling, furiously waiting for the guy to wear himself out, and fifteen minutes later he finally stopped.

But by that time Margit was wide awake, and she decided that she might as well get up. Besides, she was afraid that if she went back to sleep, she would return to that eerie wartime scene that had been one of her recurring nightmares as a kid. She hadn't had that dream in years—not until a couple of days ago, that is. And now again this morning. Even as an adult, she had to admit that the dream still terrified her. It always seemed so real.

Maybe she ought to thank the bad drummer for waking her up instead of cursing him.

Margit threw back the thin summer comforter and climbed out of bed. She halfheartedly attempted to go through her exercise routine, listening to Martha & the Vandellas singing "Heat Wave" and "Dancing in the Street," but she finally gave it up and took a hot shower instead. Then she put on some sweatpants and an old t-shirt from Santa Fe and wrapped a towel around her wet hair. She plodded barefoot through the house, switching on all the lights as she went. She was still feeling too spooked to wait another half hour for the sunrise to chase away the last remaining shadows.

In the kitchen Margit put on the teakettle and then rummaged in the cupboard for a packet of instant Swiss Miss. She had a sudden urge for a cup of hot chocolate, even though it was the middle of July. Cocoa had always been her mother's remedy for nightmares or a bad scare.

While she waited for the water to boil, Margit rubbed her hair with the towel and then absent-mindedly ran a comb through the damp strands. She was thinking about the Nordic myths she had been reading before she went to bed. Maybe it was the story of Balder's prescient dreams that had prompted her own nightmare.

According to several sources, the good and innocent god Balder began to have dreams foretelling his own death. His mother, the goddess Frigg, who was married to the mighty Odin, demanded that all of nature swear an oath, promising not to harm her son. Even the elements fire and water took the oath. Only the young and tender mistletoe was exempt. So it was this plant that the trickster god Loki used when he decided to make a spear on the sly. He then gave the weapon to Høder, who was blind, and made him pitch it unwittingly at Balder. The god was slain, and the prophecy of his dreams was fulfilled.

What a charming guy that Loki was, thought Margit as she poured hot water over the powdered cocoa and stirred briskly. A real opportunist.

She carried the steaming cup into the living room and set it on the table next to the big armchair in the corner. Feeling the need for some air, she opened a window and switched on the oscillating fan. Then she curled up in the chair and began to sip her soothing drink. She hoped that Gregor wouldn't decide to jump on the front door anytime soon and startle her. She was nervous enough as it was.

Gregor often stayed out all night in the summertime, but when he wanted back in, he would leap at the handle on the front door, hang by his paws, and kick at the door with his back feet. Margit had actually seen him do it once, and it was quite a sight. He made enough noise to be heard even in the basement library.

Margit picked up the mythology book from the table next to her chair and idly flipped through the pages. She hadn't learned anything more about the ravens. But the chapter devoted to Odin, who was the chief of the Æsir gods, had rekindled her child-hood fascination with the ancient stories. And she had ended up reading almost the entire book the night before.

She had remembered that Odin sacrificed one eye in return for knowledge, but she forgot that he was the god of occult wisdom—which he acquired by hanging for nine nights from Yggdrasil, the world tree. He was a necromancer, the god of hanged men, and the god of war. Oddly enough, he was also the god of poetry. But when the end of the world, known as "Ragnarøk," finally arrived someday, all of the dead warriors would join forces with Odin to battle a savage wolf.

Margit shook her head and smiled wryly.

The Scandinavians sure do love their gloom and doom, she thought as she stared at an illustration of the fiery cataclysm of Ragnarøk. Unlike other mythologies, the stories of the Nordic gods tended to focus more heavily on the destructive finale rather than on any life-giving cosmology.

It was only because of Thor's constant vigilance and great

strength that the monstrous demons and giants of the world could be fended off for any length of time at all.

Margit riffled through the pages of her book and stopped at the section about the wily Loki, who was inexplicably included in the upper echelon of Æsir gods, even though he was the son of a giant. He turned out to be a very bad seed—a fitting model for those who argue that innate traits are stronger than the influences of environment.

A total troublemaker, thought Margit as she again read about Loki's penchant for nasty jokes and pranks. Like all con artists, he had a certain charisma, but eventually any trace of playfulness vanished from his antics. His deceit and cunning soon proved deadly, and he became the treacherous enemy within the walls of the gods.

Loki was also a shape-changer who could even switch his sex, and he gave birth to three horrific offspring: Hel, the goddess of death; Jørmungand, the serpent encircling the world; and Fenrir, the wolf who would break loose from his chains in the Ragnarøk and wreak destruction on gods and humans alike.

Margit put down the book and closed her eyes. She was thinking that if anything could match the cruelty of Loki's deeds, it was the punishment inflicted on him by the other gods.

When they finally captured him, they bound him to a rock with the guts of his own son. Then they hung a snake above Loki's head so that the poison would drip into his mouth. His wife held a bowl under the snake to catch the drops, but whenever the bowl was full, she would have to get up to empty it. And while she was gone, the dripping poison would make Loki writhe so violently that the whole earth would shudder.

In pagan times, earthquakes were always ascribed to the convulsions of Loki struggling against his bonds. But everyone knew that one day, in the Ragnarøk, Loki would escape. And then he would join up with the evil giants to fight the gods.

That's one guy who's going to get his revenge, thought Margit, and then she drifted off into an uneasy sleep.

She was dreaming of mountains shaped like giant serpents and wolves when the piercing sound of the phone jolted her awake.

Margit groaned as she got up from the armchair and stumbled over to the end table next to the sofa to pick up the phone before her answering machine switched on. She had a severe crick in her neck, her spine felt like it was welded into a permanent "S" shape, and her left arm was completely numb.

"You're going to get all bent sleeping like that," Joe always used to warn her if it got to be too late and Margit started nodding out in her favorite reading chair. He would lift the book out of her lap, take her hand, and pull her gently to her feet. Then he would lead her into the bedroom, and they would usually end up in bed together, making love.

No use thinking about that now, Margit told herself, trying to ignore the sensation of heat that suddenly washed over her body. She missed Joe's voice. She missed his kisses and his touch. She missed the sex. Maybe she had made a terrible mistake. Maybe she should take him back.

She pushed her hair out of her eyes and glanced at the clock on the mantelpiece as she picked up the phone. It was almost eight o'clock, which meant that she'd been curled up in that chair for well over two hours. No wonder she felt stiff and creaky.

"Hello?" she said, unable to hold back a yawn.

"Ms. Andersson? Detective Tristano here. Hope I didn't get you out of bed."

Margit blinked in surprise. He was the last person she had

expected to hear from. She had a great urge to say brashly, "No, but maybe you'd like to get me *into* bed." But instead she replied demurely, "That's OK, I've been up for a while."

"Good. There are some new developments in the case that I thought you should know about. First of all, the raven card you received was sent from Vashon Island, as you thought. Since it arrived at the airport on Saturday, we know that it must have been mailed between five p.m. last Thursday and seven in the morning on Friday. If it was put in the box at any other time on Friday, it would have had a Seattle postmark on the envelope. During regular work hours, all mail from the island is sent over here to Seattle to be postmarked and distributed."

Margit slumped down on the sofa and hunched up her right shoulder to hold the phone to her ear. This didn't help the crick in her neck, but at least it freed up her hand so she could rub some life back into her numb left arm. She wondered why Tristano felt all of this was so urgent that he had to call her at eight in the morning.

"We managed to get a few good fingerprints off the card," continued the detective. "And we found a match."

"You did?" exclaimed Margit, sitting up so abruptly that the receiver fell off her shoulder. It landed on the end table with a loud clatter.

"Sorry," she told Tristano, "I dropped the phone. So who is it? Who sent the card?"

"His name is Sven Stenstrup."

"Have you arrested him?" asked Margit eagerly.

"Not exactly. But I suppose you might say that we have him in custody."

"What do you mean?" Margit could hear a slight hesitation in the detective's voice, and she wondered why he was being so evasive. There must be something he wasn't telling her. "How can you take him into custody without arresting him?"

Tristano paused for a moment and then said quietly, "Mr. Stenstrup is in the morgue."

"You mean he's dead?"

"Yes. His body was found yesterday morning, but he'd been dead for several days. The M.E. thinks he probably died sometime on Saturday. The case is under the jurisdiction of the Vashon police and the King County Sheriff. It was being investigated as a homicide resulting from a burglary attempt. There was no reason to connect it to Dr. Madsen's murder until we discovered the Vashon postmark and then matched up the victim's fingerprints with the ones on the card."

"How did he die?" asked Margit in a low voice, not sure that she really wanted to hear the answer.

"Mr. Stenstrup was killed by a sharp blow to the head. The coroner said that the impact would have instantly killed even a much younger and stronger man, and Mr. Stenstrup was seventy-eight. The murder weapon hasn't been found.

"But we did find some other interesting items among his personal effects," continued the detective somberly, "including the original note from Dr. Madsen—the one addressed to 'Muninn.'"

Margit took in a deep shuddery breath. So the murdered Sven Stenstrup was Muninn. She thought about the raven card that he had sent to her at the Star Air office, and she realized now that he must have meant it as a warning, not a threat. He was trying to warn her against someone else. Someone who had scared Rosa Nørgaard so badly that she died of fright. Someone who had pushed Gudrun Madsen to her death. And someone who had ended up killing Sven Stenstrup himself.

The thought of the three victims suddenly reminded Margit of those three bloody birds that she had seen laid out in the Frenchman's suitcase at the airport—the birds with their heads and feet intentionally cut off.

And then a chill ran down her spine as she remembered the series of phone calls she had been getting lately, with no one on the other end of the line. After Margit received the raven card, she thought maybe the calls had been another attempt by the mysterious Muninn to scare her.

But the last call had been made on Sunday afternoon—long after Sven Stenstrup was already dead.

17

Not the best place to store that kind of thing, of course," the detective was saying on the phone. "There's a lot of water damage, but we'd like you to take a look all the same. We assume that it's written in either Danish or Swedish. Would you have time to translate it today?"

Tristano paused expectantly, waiting for Margit's reply, but she had no idea what he was talking about. She was still sitting on the sofa with the receiver pressed to her ear, but she had been so immersed in her own thoughts about the events of the past week that she had totally missed what the detective was saying. And she couldn't make up her mind whether to tell him about the disturbing calls she had been getting.

But then she shook her head and chided herself for letting her imagination run wild. "Stop being so paranoid," she whispered.

"Pardon me?" said the detective.

"Oh, sorry," said Margit, feeling herself blush. "I got

distracted. But I'm not sure what we're talking about here. Could you back up a bit?"

"I was just saying that the Vashon police found what looks like an old diary hidden under the sink in Mr. Stenstrup's kitchen. It might not contain anything more exciting than those recipes and grocery lists in Dr. Madsen's notebook, but we'd still like to know what it says. Would you be willing to translate it for us?"

"Well, I have to see if the agency has other jobs lined up for me first. I might not be able to get to it today."

Margit realized that she was hedging, but she felt a sudden aversion to finding out anything more about this case. The third death had put a real damper on her curiosity, and at that moment she would have given anything to extract herself from the whole investigation.

She fervently wished that she had never let Brian talk her into taking the airport interpreter job in the first place. Then she wouldn't have seen Rosa Nørgaard screaming her way down the escalator. She wouldn't have heard those ominous last words. And she wouldn't be sitting here feeling scared in her own house on a muggy, overcast Wednesday morning.

"Why don't I just send the diary over with a courier and you can get to it as soon as you have time," said Tristano. "And don't worry about the price. We'll pay rush rates, of course. Just add it to your invoice for the other translation work."

"Fine," said Margit brusquely, annoyed that he would think she might be quibbling about the money.

Just then a loud cacophony of screeches and caws drew her attention to the open window. She took one look and jumped to her feet with a gasp.

"Margit? Are you all right?" the detective asked anxiously

on the phone. The concern in his voice made Margit's heart leap, and she was thrilled to hear him finally say her first name.

"It's OK," she hurried to reassure him. "It's just my cat, Gregor. It looks like he's caught a crow. I'd better run. But I'll get back to you after I've looked at the diary."

Margit hung up the phone and ran over to the coat closet. She found an old pair of boots to pull over her bare feet, and then she rushed out the door.

Two hours later Margit was standing at the espresso counter in the Cedar Café, telling Renny all about Gregor's big adventure.

"What a scene. You wouldn't have believed it. Six or seven crows were hopping up and down like crazy on the telephone wire above the front yard, shrieking their heads off. And Gregor was standing underneath next to the sumac bush, guarding the prey he had captured—a huge black crow."

"How on earth did Gregor manage to catch it?" asked Renny.

"I have no idea. But when I got there, it looked like he'd already taken a bite out of the back of the bird's neck. Some of the feathers were missing. The poor crow was still alive, but shaking all over. Its beak was wide open, but it couldn't make a sound, and it had a dazed look in its eye. So I ran over and picked Gregor up by the scruff of his neck and carried him into the house.

"I didn't really want to yell at him, because cats are supposed to be hunters, after all. And Gregor has been eyeing those crows for years, juddering at them from the living-room window. It must have been a dream come true when he finally managed to catch one. But I sure felt awful about that bird."

All of a sudden tears welled up in Margit's eyes and, to her astonishment, she found herself crying over the frothy cappuccino that Renny had just placed in front of her.

"Hey, what's the matter? Did the crow die?"

Margit shook her head but she couldn't manage to utter a single word. The tears just kept rolling down her cheeks.

"This is about something else, isn't it? C'mon, girl, you'd better sit down." And Renny led Margit over to a corner table, away from the stares of the other customers in the café.

"Now tell me what's going on."

So Margit told her friend all about the latest developments in the murder investigation, which now involved three deaths. She also mentioned the upsetting phone calls and confessed to her own misgivings about going back to the airport. But she didn't say anything about Sven Stenstrup's diary, which had arrived by messenger just as she was leaving the house.

Margit had stuck the small package in her bag, planning to look at it later in the day, after she picked up a job from the Koivisto Translation Agency. Liisa had called her at nine o'clock about translating a stack of documents that had something to do with carpet manufacturing. Apparently there were charts and photographs that couldn't be faxed, so Liisa had asked Margit to drive over and get the original documents from the office.

"Thank God I stopped in here first," she told Renny now as she wiped her eyes with a paper napkin. The talk with her friend, combined with the strong coffee, had done Margit good. She was feeling more like herself again. "It would have been embarrassing to burst into tears in front of Liisa."

"Well, you can cry on my shoulder any time you like," said Renny warmly, patting Margit's hand. "Now you take my advice and tell Alex about getting those phone calls. Maybe it's just someone dialing the wrong number. Maybe it's nothing. But you need to let the police decide whether it's something to worry about or not."

Margit nodded. Renny was right. She would mention the calls when she reported to the detective about her translation of the diary.

"And call in sick tomorrow," Renny continued. "I'm sure that the Star Air 'coach' can get along just fine without an interpreter on his team for one day. This whole business is stressing you out. And if you're already having the willies about going to the airport, then you shouldn't go. You need to listen to your instincts, girl. Sometimes fear is the best response—it can stop you from making stupid mistakes. It can even save your life."

Margit nodded again, even though she thought Renny was being a little extreme. And she was already feeling silly about mentioning her anxieties. Margit told herself that she was just overreacting because too many shocking things had been happening lately, and she was clearly on emotional overload. Breaking up with Joe had put her in a vulnerable state during the past few months. And this morning's eerie nightmare, followed by the news of another murder, certainly hadn't helped matters.

Margit appreciated Renny's advice, but she was both too conscientious and too stubborn to shirk her obligations. And as a freelancer with no regular paycheck, she never liked to turn down work.

"Well, thanks for the advice," she said with a grateful smile. "But I'd better get going now. Liisa's probably wondering what happened to me."

"OK, kiddo. Don't work too hard today. Try to relax," said Renny, getting up to give Margit a hug. Then she insisted on making her friend another cappuccino "on the house," and she handed Margit a scone to take along in the car.

"I didn't know that Bob baked scones," said Margit.

"He doesn't. He finally decided that he was tired of getting up at three a.m. to bake muffins and croissants for the morning crowd. He said he'd rather sleep in and leave the baking to someone else. So he's been trying out different suppliers. These scones are from a great place over in Issaquah—the Three Crown Bakery."

Margit was halfway across the West Seattle Bridge before she realized that she'd heard that name before.

"Of course!" she cried, slapping her hand against the steering wheel. Now she remembered quite clearly. It was at the airport last Thursday, when she was interpreting for that young Swedish man who was denied entry. The letter she had translated was a job offer from the Three Crown Bakery, signed by a Göran Hultén. And that was the same distinctive signature that had caught her eye in the guest book at Gudrun Madsen's memorial service the day before.

How curious that his name would come up on both occasions. But the Scandinavian community was a tight-knit group, and Dr. Madsen's funeral had attracted a large crowd.

Then Margit wondered whether Mr. Hultén might have decided to show up at the airport to meet his new baker in person last Thursday. If so, maybe he saw or heard something that would be useful to the investigation.

Or maybe he's the murderer, thought Margit suddenly with a shiver. If he was at the airport, maybe *he* was the man that Rosa meant when she cried "Not him!" Maybe *he* was the one who pushed Dr. Madsen out of a fifth-floor window. She had read somewhere that killers often stayed close to the scene of the crime, but would he be bold enough to attend his victim's funeral? Was it his way of taunting the police?

Margit picked up the car phone and dialed the homicide department, but Tristano and Silikov were both unavailable. She decided to call back later instead of trying to explain things on their voice mail. Or maybe she would just forget it. She was starting to think that it wasn't much of a lead anyway—merely her own speculations based on an odd coincidence that would probably sound preposterous to the detectives.

Stop scaring yourself over nothing, she told herself impatiently. You're just a little overwrought today.

On impulse Margit decided to call up the bakery. It wouldn't hurt to ask one of the employees whether Göran Hultén was at the airport on Thursday—just for her own peace of mind. And she didn't have to give her name. If the baker took the call himself, she would simply hang up.

She picked up the car phone again, got the bakery's number from directory assistance, and then dialed the new Issaquah area code followed by the seven digits.

Pretty soon we're all going to have numbers a mile long, thought Margit, shaking her head.

To her relief, a young woman answered the phone.

Margit decided the best approach was to dispense with any explanations and get right to the point. She reminded herself of the polite but authoritative tone that Inspector Tyler always used when he was questioning passengers in the Immigration area at the airport. Summoning her most professional-sounding voice she said, "I understand that you hired a baker's apprentice from Linköping, and I was wondering whether Mr. Hultén went out to pick him up at the airport last Thursday."

"No, no. That was all a big misunderstanding," the woman rushed to explain. "The Swedish guy wasn't actually going to *work* here—it was just an internship, not a real job. We weren't going to *pay* him anything. He said he just wanted to learn something about the business while he was here on vacation, so we offered to show him the ropes—as a favor to his cousin, Ulf, who used to work here. But *he's* not Swedish—he's American."

The bakery employee obviously thought Margit was actually connected with the Immigration authorities. She decided not to dissuade her of the misconception.

"We just wanted to know whether Mr. Hultén was at Sea-Tac to meet the young man," said Margit again.

"No, he was here at the bakery all day. We're remodeling and expanding into the space next door, so the boss spends all his time supervising the work. But we heard about the whole story from Ulf after he went to the airport to pick up his cousin."

"Would that be Ulf Hansson?" asked Margit, guessing that his last name might be the same as that of his Swedish cousin.

"Yes, that's right."

"And do you happen to know where we might get hold of him?"

"Well, I think he just moved, and I don't know his new number, but he works at a bar in Belltown called the Retrograde. He's not in any trouble, is he?"

"No, we'd just like to ask him a few questions. Thanks for your cooperation. You've been most helpful."

Margit hung up, feeling rather smug about her performance. Now she could cross off Göran Hultén as a possible suspect since he wasn't at the airport when Rosa Nørgaard died, and she was convinced that the murderer was there that day. But at least she had the name of someone who was on the scene: Ulf Hansson.

There was no reason to believe that he was involved in the deaths in any way. Margit wasn't about to let herself jump to any more wild conclusions. But she thought it was possible that he might have witnessed something that he didn't even know was important.

151

A few minutes later Margit lucked out and found a parking spot right in front of the translation agency. As she climbed the stairs to the second-floor office, she decided to walk over to the Retrograde after she picked up her job. It was only a few blocks away. She had driven past the place many times, although she'd never been inside. But now she thought she might just drop by and ask Ulf Hansson a few questions after all.

18

Six hours later Margit copied her file to a disk and then clicked on the icon for her email program. She gave a big sigh as she stood up to stretch her back while she waited for the mail to download.

She now knew more than she ever wanted to know about Danish carpet technology, including the comparative advantages of hydrophobic versus hydrophilic fibers. There were still over sixty pages left to translate, but at least she had deciphered most of the industry jargon, and she was beginning to pick up speed. She had also compiled a lengthy new glossary to add to her collection of technical terms used by specific businesses.

Glossaries were essential tools for professional translators, since it was impossible to remember specialized vocabulary from job to job. Months or even years might go by before the same topic came up again. And like most of her colleagues, Margit had trained herself to forget about a job once it was finished and out the door.

"Unless the subject interests me, I don't need all that excess data cluttering up my brain," Margit recalled telling Brian only a few weeks ago. "Especially if it's something tedious, like the facts in a corporate annual report. Or something gross, like the details in that medical manual I did. If I had to remember everything I translated about ringworm, lockjaw, or salmonella, I'd probably end up totally paranoid about germs. I'd have to seal up all the windows, nail shut the door, and never go out again."

Brian had laughed and said, "Good thing you never wanted to be a doctor."

The word "doctor" brought Margit's thoughts right back to the murder investigation, which she had purposely pushed out of her mind while she was working on the translation job.

As she sat down in front of her computer again, she couldn't help replaying the conversation she'd had with Ulf Hansson earlier in the day, wondering if she might have missed something.

After picking up her job at the agency, Margit had walked down the street toward the Retrograde, passing one swank boutique after another. The clouds had finally dispersed, and the morning sun was glinting off all the windows in the plethora of new highrises. The Belltown area north of downtown used to be a ragtag collection of old brick apartment buildings, smoky taverns, storefront missions, and the offices of various trade unions. But the place had gone upscale over the past five years, as one block after another was demolished to make room for towering new condominiums. And rents had simultaneously soared. Lately Liisa had even started threatening to move the agency to Kent, where office space was still cheap.

When Margit finally reached the Retrograde and stepped inside, she thought for a moment that she had stumbled into a museum or a movie set instead of a bar. The decor of the place was totally devoted to memorabilia from the sixties and early seventies.

Every inch of wall space was covered with framed psyche-delic posters from legendary rock concerts. An old jukebox in mint condition offered a selection of 45s with hits by Hendrix, CSNY, and the Jefferson Airplane. But the volume had been turned down so low that Country Joe's "I-Feel-Like-I'm-Fixin'-to-Die Rag" sounded as tepid as Muzak. An eight-dollar ticket from Woodstock had been encased in glass and was hanging next to a certificate of authentication. Lava lamps stood on all the tables, which were neatly decorated with Day-Glo flower decals. And off to the left, life-size cutouts of Janis Joplin and Jim Morrison identified the ladies' and men's rooms, respectively.

Margit found the whole place both disconcerting and dis-tasteful. It made her feel old to see familiar items from her teen-age years so meticulously preserved and displayed—as if they were some kind of archeological artifacts. And she was frankly appalled to see the trappings of that turbulent era suddenly re-discovered and deemed "retro chic."

A woman wearing a halter top, brand-new bellbottoms, and chunky platform shoes was sitting at one of the tables with an empty espresso cup in front of her. She was reading a copy of the latest hip rag called *The Stranger*, which for some reason Margit always misread as the "Strangler." But there were no other cus-tomers, since it was a little too early for the lunch crowd.

A tall man in his mid-twenties, wearing a tie-dyed shirt, was standing behind the bar at the far end of the room with his eyes fixed on the TV hanging from the ceiling. He was watching a baseball game, which seemed as incongruous a choice as a war movie would have been in that setting.

Margit walked over, sat down on a stool, and ordered a glass of mineral water with lemon.

"Hey, aren't you Ulf Hansson?" she asked, feigning surprise as she handed the young man a five.

"Uh-huh," he said, as he quickly counted out her change and then turned his attention back to the game. His dark hair was cut short and slicked back with gel. He had a striking face— long and lean, with a high forehead, prominent cheekbones, and an ivory complexion. And he had the most startling blue eyes that Margit had ever seen.

"Maybe you don't remember me, but I saw you at the airport the other day when I was interpreting for your cousin Pär in Immigration," she lied. She hadn't actually seen him there at all.

Ulf finally tore himself away from the TV and gave Margit a long hard stare with those piercing blue eyes of his.

"Oh yeah?" he said doubtfully. "What a joke that whole thing was. I couldn't believe those jerks wouldn't at least let him stay for a few days. After he flew all that way to get here."

Margit shook her head sympathetically and then asked, "Did you happen to see the old woman who fell on the escalator?"

"Sure. I was standing right up against the glass in the viewing area, wondering where Pär had gone because he never came out of Customs with the other passengers on his flight. And then I heard this muffled screaming, so I looked up and saw that old woman waving her arms around and going berserk. And then she fell at the bottom of the escalator."

Ulf paused for a moment, and then snapped his fingers. "Now I remember. You were the one who rushed over and dragged her away from the crowd. Whatever happened to her, anyway?"

"She died," said Margit somberly. "A heart attack. But we couldn't locate any of her friends or family members. Did you notice anyone who seemed to be waiting for her?"

"No, not really. I saw a man and a woman in the crowd nearby who acted awfully upset, but they were speaking Danish and I couldn't make out what they were saying. The Danes always swallow their words. And I have a hard enough time understanding Swedish when my relatives start talking too fast—especially my grandfather."

Margit suddenly remembered that she still had the program from Gudrun Madsen's funeral in her bag. She pulled out the rose-colored paper, unfolded it, and then placed it on the bar. "Is this the woman you saw?" she asked Ulf, pointing to the doctor's picture on the front.

He studied the photo for a moment and then said, "Yeah, I think it might be." Then he took another look at the program and asked Margit with surprise, "But why does it say 'In memoriam'? Is *she* dead too?"

"Yes, unfortunately she is. Dr. Madsen was murdered last Thursday night, only a matter of hours after you saw her at the airport. Didn't you read the news about the Queen Anne murder?"

"Naw. But I never pay much attention to the local news—not even on the tube. Too much crap going on in this town."

Margit nodded in agreement, took a sip of her mineral water, and then asked, "Did you notice anything else about Dr. Madsen and her companion?"

Ulf Hansson shook his head. "Not really. My grandfather came over to the viewing area just then and asked me what was going on. I remember seeing the couple glance in our direction, and then they both took off fast, heading downstairs. I didn't notice where they went because a minute later an Immigration officer came out to tell us that Pär had to go back to Sweden. But if they were waiting for the woman who died, didn't they get in touch with the authorities?"

"No, apparently they didn't. That's what's so strange."

"How come you're so interested in this whole thing, anyway. Are you a cop?" Ulf asked, suddenly suspicious.

"No, not at all. I'm just an interpreter. But it was pretty

upsetting to have that old woman die right in front of me, and it seemed so odd that she didn't have anyone waiting for her. And then when I came in here and recognized you from the airport, I just thought you might have seen or heard something while you were waiting for your cousin."

Ulf seemed satisfied with Margit's reply, even though she hadn't explained a few things — such as how she knew that Gudrun Madsen was at the airport that day. Or why she happened to be carrying around a program from Dr. Madsen's funeral in her bag.

"Did you say that your grandfather was there too?" she asked now.

"Yeah, he drove out to the airport with me. He's been visiting my folks for a few weeks — from Germany. Actually, what used to be East Germany. It's his first time here since the Wall fell."

"Do you think he might have seen something?"

"Naw, I doubt it. He missed all the excitement because he was back in the main terminal, looking at those two old fighter planes they have on display. I don't think he even made it out to the South Satellite until after the old woman collapsed."

Then Margit couldn't think of anything else to ask, so she finished her mineral water and got up to leave. "Well, thanks for answering my questions," she said.

"No problem," said Ulf with a shrug, his eyes already flitting back to the ball game on TV.

And then Margit walked back to her car, glad to escape the oppressively trendy atmosphere of the Retrograde, but disappointed that the encounter hadn't proved more enlightening.

Now, sitting in front of her computer and reading her email, Margit felt vaguely uneasy. There was something about the conversation with Ulf Hansson that bothered her, but she couldn't figure out what it was.

Impatiently, she shook back her hair and scanned the remaining email messages. She was surprised to find one from her father. When he was still teaching, he used to send her email all the time—brief messages written when he could grab a free moment at work. But ever since he retired, he had taken to calling her instead. These days he only used email for news that was too trivial to discuss in a phone conversation. But this message turned out to be far from trivial.

"*Kära* Margit," she read. "Maybe it would be best if you didn't mention what we talked about on the phone yesterday to your mother. Janna always likes telling people that you were named after a famous author, and I don't really want to disillusion her after all these years. And you know how sensitive she is about any talk of the war. I'm sure she hasn't told you why. But since the subject has come up and I've already revealed one secret, I thought I might as well tell you what happened to your mother. I think you're entitled to know. But let's keep this between us."

Margit's eyes widened as she stared at the screen. Then she quickly pressed on the arrow key to scroll down to the next paragraph.

"Janna had just turned eleven when she witnessed one of the worst catastrophes of the war in Denmark. It was on March 21, 1945, and she was home alone that day, recuperating from a bad cold. Her father was at work, her two brothers were in school, and her mother had gone into town because there were rumors that a shop over in Nørrebro had gotten in a new shipment of shoes, which were hard to come by at the time.

"Janna was lying in bed reading a book in their apartment

on Maglekildevej in Frederiksberg when she heard the sound of approaching planes in the distance. She thought about going downstairs to the basement shelter, but since the air raid sirens hadn't sounded, she stayed where she was. A few minutes later, all hell broke loose."

Margit jabbed at the arrow key and scrolled down to the next paragraph, holding her breath. The phone started ringing, but she decided to ignore it this time and let her answering machine take the call.

"The RAF had planned a daring attack on Gestapo headquarters in Shellhuset in the middle of Copenhagen. On that March morning the raid was brilliantly carried out, and the first wave of bombers successfully destroyed the target. But an unforeseeable accident resulted in terrible consequences. The planes caught the Germans by surprise because they came in at rooftop level. That's why the air raid sirens gave no warning until bombs started to fall. But on the way into the city, one of the first planes hit a signal tower, swerved off course, and crashed near the French School in Frederiksberg. When the pilots in the second and third waves of bombers saw the smoke, they mistakenly assumed it was the target, so that's where they dropped their bombs. Over a hundred people were killed—most of them children at the school. And hundreds more were wounded. Janna had crawled under her bed to wait out the attack, and she was lucky to escape unharmed. Her apartment building was badly damaged, but it was one of the few that didn't go up in flames.

"Your mother has never told me what she saw when she and her neighbors finally crept out of the building and surveyed the devastation all around. But I've seen photographs, and it must have been a horrific sight, especially for a child. That's why she never wants to talk about the war. I think she's still trying to wipe that day out of her memory."

Margit stared at the words on the screen, shuddering at the thought of her mother living through such a terrifying experience all alone, and at the young age of eleven. "My God," she whispered, shaking her head.

She wrote a brief reply to her father, thanking him for telling her Janna's story, since it was something that had always puzzled her. And she promised not to say anything about it to her mother. Then Margit switched off the computer and stood up.

"Time for dinner," she called to Gregor. She was beginning to feel lightheaded from lack of food, and her muscles were aching from sitting in one spot too long. A nice plate of pasta and a glass of wine should fix her right up. Later that evening she would have to tackle Sven Stenstrup's diary, which she still hadn't looked at. But she couldn't put it off any longer.

Before she went out to the kitchen, Margit pressed the button on her answering machine to play back the phone message that had come in while she was reading her father's email. She stood there for a good two minutes, still thinking about her mother's wartime experience, before she realized that she was listening to the faint sound of someone breathing. Then there was a sharp click on the tape, and the line went dead.

19

Thanks for letting me stay here tonight," said Margit as she served up two plates of linguini with marinara sauce. Then she set them on Renny's kitchen table and sat down across from her friend.

"Hey, I'm glad you're here. What are friends for, anyway?" said Renny, sprinkling a light dusting of parmesan cheese over her pasta. "Besides, it's a treat to have someone else cook for me. You can stay here as long as you like."

Margit smiled, grateful to be sitting in Renny's large, airy kitchen. It almost made her forget about the menacing phone calls and the recent murders.

The room was painted a deep yellow with white trim, and a lush flower garden was visible through the open back door. The wall next to the table was covered with framed photographs of Renny's extended family. There were also a few photos of the painters that she especially admired, including Jacob Lawrence and Georgia O'Keeffe. On the opposite wall hung a series of colorful lithographs that Renny had done a few years back. Tacked up next to the refrigerator were glitzy postcards from

Scotland, India, and Japan sent by her lover, who was an art dealer. And a bright poster for a Matisse exhibition was taped to one of the cupboards.

Renny took a piece of garlic bread from the basket on the table and said, "I'm just glad you called me instead of spending the whole night feeling scared. Are you sure you don't want to bring Gregor over here too?"

"No, he doesn't like to leave his territory. I didn't want to lock him up in the house, but he'll be fine outdoors. He's used to staying out all night when it's hot like this."

"So what did Alex say when you told him about the phone calls?"

"He said the police would put a tap on my phone, and I actually thought he sounded a little worried. Then he got all stuffy and stern, and he practically ordered me to spend a few days with a friend."

"But he didn't invite you over to *his* place?" asked Renny with a grin.

"Very funny," said Margit.

At first she had refused to listen to Tristano. His brusque tone of voice had made her stubborn—she never responded well to being ordered to do anything. In fact, Margit had told the detective quite firmly that she wasn't about to be chased out of her own house. But after she hung up the phone, she realized suddenly that she was shivering all over, even though it was 78 degrees.

That's when Margit decided to ask Renny if she could spend the night in her guest room. No sense in pretending that the phone calls didn't bother her, although she was a little embarrassed by her reaction. But by tomorrow Margit expected to have regained her equilibrium enough to go back home.

"So, do you think you'll be all right here by yourself? You

really don't mind if I go?" asked Renny now, giving her friend a worried look.

"Of course I'll be all right. You can't cancel your drawing class just because of me. Your students wouldn't be happy. And besides, I'm going to be busy myself—I brought along my laptop so I could work on a translation job tonight."

Half an hour later Renny dashed off to her class, calling over her shoulder, "Thanks for fixing dinner, kiddo. I should be back around eleven, but don't wait up."

Margit wiped off the table with a damp sponge, switched on the dishwasher, and tucked the evening paper under her arm as she left the kitchen.

All the other rooms on the ground floor of Renny's house had been turned into one vast studio, with canvases stacked against the walls everywhere and several half-finished paintings sitting on easels. Sketchbooks were piled up on the floor next to stacks of art books. Dozens of baskets held tubes of paint, while a multitude of large tin cans and pottery crocks held brushes of all different sizes. As Margit headed up the stairs, she studied the new drawings pinned up along the wall. They all showed the same male nude, but each one had been sketched from a slightly different angle.

Every time she visited Renny, Margit realized that she was getting a rare glimpse into the workings of an artist's creative imagination. Most people only saw the finished work of a painter hanging neatly in a gallery or a museum. But in Renny's studio she was allowed to see the practice sketches—all those repeated attempts to capture a particular curve in the back, a ripple of muscle, or a singular facial expression. And Margit was always impressed with Renny's sheer tenacity—her willingness to work through an idea or an emotion or a dream, sketching the image over and over until she finally got it right.

At the top of the stairs, Margit turned left and went into the guest room. With a sigh she dropped into the oversized armchair near the window and spread the newspaper on her lap.

The article about Sven Stenstrup's death gave some details about the victim, but there was no photograph. The reporter was obviously more interested in the shock caused by the rare event of a murder in the laid-back community of Vashon Island.

Stenstrup was described as a taciturn man who had built his modest house on a secluded, wooded lot in the 1950s after he emigrated to Vashon from Denmark. Margit noted with interest that he was originally from Snekkersten, a fishing village just south of Helsingør. His wife, a nurse from Seattle, had died over a decade ago. At the time of his death, Sven Stenstrup was apparently still making a small living as a handyman, working for his island neighbors. Several people who were interviewed by the reporter said that he was an excellent carpenter and that he could fix just about anything. Every morning he went to the library to read the newspapers, and that's where people contacted him if they needed some work done, since he didn't have a telephone. But he did have a rather expensive assortment of short-wave radio equipment, some of which was missing when his body was discovered.

Detective Tristano had told Margit on the phone that the police now thought the equipment might have been stolen to divert the investigation from the real motive behind the murder—a motive that somehow linked three deaths.

Margit tossed the newspaper onto the floor. OK, quit procrastinating, she told herself.

From the table next to her chair she picked up the small package that had been delivered to her house that morning. She unwrapped the paper and pulled out a battered-looking book. The gray cardboard cover was splotched and water-stained, and moisture had made the pages buckle and swell. Some of them seemed to be stuck together, and it would take some delicate prying to separate them without tearing the paper.

The blue ink on most of the pages was badly streaked, turning the text into an illegible blur. But here and there Margit could make out a few Danish words or even a whole line. And as she read, a feeling of excitement began to come over her.

After a few minutes, she got up and moved to the desk in the corner so she could type the translation into her laptop as she went along. She ended up with a short list of phrases:

made exchange at 2 (3?) a.m.
ten travelers and one messenger
Kronborg
major repairs
hid them in summerhouse for two days until boat ready
six travelers safely across
lunch packet delivered
O. unhappy with the rendezvous site
fifteen thousand kroner
wants more money
sailing ship damaged, another delay
R. has contact we might be able to use and will bring him over tomorrow
no word yet and H. still not back

"Wow," whispered Margit. "So I was right all along."

Here was the connection that they had been looking for. There were no dates or places named other than Hamlet's castle, but it seemed obvious that the diary must have been written during the war. And it seemed equally clear that Sven Stenstrup had been involved in the illegal Øresund traffic, taking refugees and couriers across to Sweden. Given his knack for fixing things, maybe he was responsible for keeping the boats seaworthy. Or maybe his interest in shortwave equipment dated back to the war, when radio communication must have played a vital role.

Margit wondered what Stenstrup meant by a "lunch packet," and who "O." might be. But she had no doubt that the "H." and "R." in his diary referred to Gudrun Madsen (or Huginn) and Rosa Nørgaard.

The middle section of the book was so water-damaged that Margit could decipher only the word "Swedish" and a single sentence: "L. working with group now." The initial "L." then showed up several more times. She also managed to spell out an odd phrase: "more cleaning murders," but she had no idea what the context was.

The last section had been written in pencil, so it was actually still legible. It contained long lists of numbers that seemed to be bookkeeping entries showing credits and debits. Items in the plus column were labeled: transport payment, transfer fee, and miscellaneous. The minus side showed: fuel, skipper's pay, food, supplies, and quite a few entries followed by a question mark.

When Margit came to the last page of the book, she suddenly found an entire paragraph intact.

"All of us in agreement, although it took a lot of work to convince H. Still doesn't want to believe that L. is responsible. Letting personal feelings cloud the facts. Constant shortfalls over the past few months. And now this. It has to be him. The evidence is irrefutable. No other explanation possible. Steps must be taken. We'll have to do it soon, before L. catches on."

Margit gave a long, low whistle. So the large sums of money must have proved too tempting for one of the members of the group—someone that Gudrun Madsen felt so strongly about that she didn't want to accept the "evidence." And from the sinister tone of the last lines, it looked as if the embezzler L. was in for big trouble.

A rustling sound outside the window made Margit glance up with a start, but it was only the wind jostling the branches of a nearby pine tree. It was past nine o'clock but still quite light outside. Margit turned her attention back to her laptop. In her mind, she slowly began to piece together a plausible scenario, based on the phrases from the diary and everything else she had learned during the past week.

But there were still some things she didn't understand, so she decided to give Egon Kirkeby a call. Maybe he could answer her questions.

Back downstairs in Renny's kitchen, Margit reached for the wall phone and dialed Egon's number. As she waited for him to answer, she leaned against the counter and absent-mindedly stared at the family photos hanging on the wall. If it weren't for the old-fashioned clothes and hairstyle, she could have sworn that she was looking at Renny standing proudly in front of a brand-new Model T. But it was actually a picture of her great-aunt, taken back in the 1920s in Chicago. The family resemblance was uncanny.

Margit shifted the receiver to her other hand and yawned. It had been a long day, starting with the rude awakening by the bad drummer at five a.m. Maybe she should go to bed and try to call Egon in the morning. But at that moment he finally picked up the phone.

"It's funny, but I was just sitting here reading about the Vashon murder in the paper," he told Margit as soon as she explained why she was calling. "And when I saw that Sven Stenstrup was from Snekkersten, I wondered if there might be some connection."

"Why's that?"

"Because it was another one of the ports often used by the Øresund groups."

"Is that right?" said Margit, certain now that she was on the right track. "Well, the police found an old diary from the war in his house, and they asked me to translate it. Most of it is impossible to decipher. I could only figure out a few phrases, and they don't all make sense. I was wondering if I could read them to you, and you could tell me what you think."

"By all means," said Egon, sounding intrigued.

So Margit slowly read off the list of phrases. When she came to the reference to a "lunch packet," Egon chuckled.

"Do you know what that means?" she asked him.

"Yes, I do. All kinds of messages were constantly being sent back and forth across Øresund by courier. If they weren't conveyed verbally, then they were often written out on the thin little slips of paper that Danes put in between their open-faced sandwiches. A lunch packet actually made an excellent hiding place—although I can remember getting a few 'ripe' messages that had been layered on top of some smelly cheese."

Margit read the rest of the list and then asked Egon what a "cleaning murder" was.

"You must mean '*clearing* murder,'" he said, his voice no

longer sounding amused. "It was another despicable policy introduced by Hitler late in the war to try and curtail the growing resistance in Denmark. He had already ordered that every act of sabotage against the occupying forces would be met with a counterattack. If the Danes blew up a railroad line, the Nazis would blow up a restaurant or a store, hoping to turn the people against the resistance movement by endangering the lives of ordinary citizens. We called these retaliatory acts of sabotage 'Schalburgtage'—named after the Schalburg Corps, the Danish SS."

Egon paused for a long moment, and Margit assumed that he was caught up in memories of his own wartime experiences. "And was that the same thing as a 'clearing murder'?" she prodded him gently.

"No. Near the end of 1943, Hitler also ordered that every time an informer was liquidated by the resistance, the Germans would select and execute a prominent Dane. They made their choice of victims based on advice from the security police and other sources. The first such 'clearing murder' was carried out on January 4, 1944."

"Why does that date sound so familiar?" wondered Margit.

"That was the day Kaj Munk was murdered."

"Oh, that's right," she said soberly, remembering her literary history. Munk was a forty-six-year-old Lutheran minister who was well-known in Denmark as a controversial poet and playwright. During the occupation he used both his pulpit and his pen to speak out against the Nazis. On that infamous winter morning in 1944, he was seized in his home, taken to a road near Silkeborg, and shot dead in a grove of trees.

Margit still didn't know why the term "clearing murder" had turned up in Sven Stenstrup's diary, but at least she could use it as a means of dating the entry. It must have been written sometime after January 1944, since the phrase wouldn't have been in common use before then.

"The Germans and their cohorts probably committed over a hundred 'clearing murders' in Denmark before the war ended," Egon continued. "But I remember there was one other case that got a lot of attention."

"What happened?" asked Margit.

"Well, I think it was in early July of 1944. An informer was killed in Roskilde, and the next night the Germans took their retribution. But this time there were two victims instead of one. Two highly respected citizens were found shot outside their homes in Copenhagen. And both of them were doctors."

20

At 7:15 on Thursday morning Margit fumbled for the "off" button on the alarm clock, which was loudly buzzing on the bedside table.

Just five more minutes and I'll get up, she promised herself groggily, turning onto her side.

She was dreaming that Joe was stroking her hair and whispering in her ear. He was running the fingers of his right hand down her spine and along her bare flank. He was making her skin tingle and her toes curl. He was nibbling on her earlobe and kissing her shoulder. He was making her shiver and sigh. She wrapped her arms tighter around Joe's warm body and snuggled her face in the crook of his neck.

Then Margit woke up.

She was clutching a down pillow to her breast, her legs were tangled up in the sheet, and a breeze from the open window was blowing gently across her bare skin.

Margit rolled onto her back and stared glumly at the sun-filled room, disappointed at finding herself alone and perplexed by the unfamiliar setting. Finally she realized that she was lying in the comfortable bed in Renny's guest room—and then she remembered why she was there.

A persistent ticking sound made Margit turn her head to the left. Mickey Mouse was grinning at her gleefully from the clock face, pointing his white-gloved hands at the 12 and the 8.

"Oh shit," muttered Margit. How could she have let herself oversleep? She had to be on the road to the airport by 8:45. The first charter flight wasn't due in until 10:30, but she was expected to be there an hour ahead of time to listen to the station manager's "pre-game" pep talk. And Brian liked to go over the passenger list with her before the arrival. The drive to Sea-Tac from West Seattle took a good half hour, and finding a parking place in the crowded airport garage would take another ten minutes.

Margit glanced at the clock again. It was going to be tight. And now there was no time to call Detective Tristano and tell him about the diary and her conversation with Egon Kirkeby. It would just have to wait until later in the day.

She had brought along her work clothes, but she would still have to stop by her own house to feed Gregor and to check for faxes from the translation agency. She just hoped there wouldn't be any more eerie phone messages waiting for her.

With a groan Margit jumped out of bed and ran down the hall to the bathroom to take a quick shower. Half an hour later she was dressed and out the door, although her hair was still damp. She unlocked the Mazda, tossed her overnight bag onto the passenger seat, and got in. As she drove the five blocks to her house, she blessed Renny for leaving her a thermos of coffee.

By the time Renny came back from her class the night before, Margit had been sound asleep, so they didn't get a chance to talk. When Renny left for her shift at the Cedar Café around six that morning, she must have assumed that Margit was planning to take her advice and call in sick. She left a blueberry muffin and a bowl of fruit on the kitchen table. Propped up against the thermos was a note that said: "Enjoy your day off."

"As if I could afford a day off," grumbled Margit as she pulled into her driveway, grabbed her bag, and jumped out of the car.

Gregor was standing in the front yard, hissing at a cream-colored cat who was nonchalantly making his morning rounds through the neighborhood. When Margit rushed up the path toward the house, Gregor backed away from his opponent and then turned and raced up the stairs to the front door.

"Why can't you be friends with that sweet old cat?" Margit said as they entered the house together. She dropped her bag on the floor and strode into the kitchen to give Gregor some food. Then she left him there, hunkered down in front of his dish, crunching contentedly. He would be happy to spend the day curled up on the sofa after being outdoors all night.

Margit went into her study, snatched several pages out of the fax tray, and noted with relief that there were no new phone messages. Then she dashed out of the house, calling goodbye to Gregor as she left.

She decided to take 509 instead of I-5. It was a slightly longer route to the airport from West Seattle, but it was actually sometimes faster because the traffic was less intense.

As Margit drove along West Marginal Way, she listened to a soothing tape of Michael Franks and drank two cups of coffee from Renny's thermos. By the time she reached the entrance to 509, she was feeling more alert and ready to look at the faxes she had brought along. Keeping one eye on the road, Margit skimmed the first page, expecting it to be about a translation job from Liisa. But the message was typed on official SPD stationery, and it said:

> Dear Ms. Andersson,
> I attach two faxes from the Copenhagen police. We would appreciate your help in translating the Danish article.
> Sincerely,
> Detective Ed Silikov

Margit slipped the page behind the other two and then read the first fax from the Danish police.

Written in understandable but not entirely correct English, the letter advised Detective Silikov that there was still no trace of any relatives of Rosa Nørgaard, either in Denmark or Sweden. Her husband had died in the 1960s, she had no children, and she had never remarried. They knew only that she was a retired schoolteacher who lived alone. Her neighbors and the local shopkeepers couldn't tell the police much, although they had all noticed that Fru Nørgaard seemed to be acting a little strange lately. A search of her small apartment in Frederiksberg had turned up nothing of interest. But yesterday the Danish police had discovered a safe-deposit box in her name, which contained a rather substantial amount of cash in very old bills. It also contained the attached clipping. The police had no idea whether it would be relevant to the Seattle investigation, but they had decided to forward it just the same.

Before Margit could read the third fax, her attention was diverted by a red minitruck that refused to get off her tail. Apparently 70 mph wasn't fast enough for the guy, so she finally changed lanes to let him by. The driver jammed his hand on the horn as he roared past and then flipped her the finger out the window.

"What an idiot," snapped Margit, but she restrained her own urge to return the gesture. Road rage was nothing to be trifled with these days, as Bob was always reminding his customers at the Cedar Café. It was one of his biggest gripes lately, and he was fond of rattling off statistics about the increasing number of drivers brandishing guns on the roads around Seattle. He had even printed up a bumper sticker that said "Don't be a fool—stay cool."

Margit glanced at her watch with a frown and then went back to reading the faxes as she drove.

The last one turned out to be a photocopy of two brief newspaper articles from 1944, printed side by side. The first column reported the death of a tobacconist named S.V. Nielsen in Roskilde. An alleged informer, he was shot down in front of his store as he arrived for work on the morning of July 6th. There were no witnesses, or at least none willing to come forward to speak to the authorities.

The headline of the second column said: "Respected Physicians Killed." The article reported that Dr. Jens Bjørnsen and Dr. Morten Pedersen were found dead in front of their homes on the night of July 7th. Both had been shot through the head. The term "clearing murder" wasn't used, but the article strongly implied that the shootings were acts of revenge, undoubtedly instigated by agents of the occupying power. The rest of the article praised the esteemed doctors for their work at the State University Hospital in Copenhagen and then gave details of the funeral arrangements.

Margit shook her head in amazement as she dropped the faxes onto the passenger seat beside her. Here was an actual account of the event that Egon Kirkeby had mentioned on the phone the night before. And it was apparently so important to Rosa Nørgaard that she had kept the clipping and hidden it away all these years.

As Margit changed lanes again to pass an old VW bus that was chugging along at 40 mph, she thought about the cash found in Rosa's safe-deposit box. She wasn't sure how that money fit in with everything else she was starting to piece together about the case. Impatiently, Margit ran her hand through her hair as she went over her theory one more time. Then she switched off the tape deck so she could concentrate better.

The whole investigation had started with the discovery of the copper coin near Gudrun Madsen's body—a coin that was used during the war to warn of the presence of an informer.

She wondered whether this had anything to do with the man called L. in Sven Stenstrup's diary. Maybe the embezzler L. was looking for other lucrative ways to make money, and so he offered his services to the Germans as an informer. Since he was a member of one of the Øresund groups, he would be in a position to pass along highly useful information and demand a good price. But he wouldn't inform on his own group, because that would jeopardize his chances of continuing to rake in the dough—both by siphoning off route funds and by gathering more information to sell to the Nazis.

Margit took the airport exit from 509 and slowed to a stop at the intersection to wait for the light to change.

She was thinking about Gudrun Madsen, trying to picture her as a young woman who was brave enough to risk her life working for the resistance—and impetuous enough to fall in love with someone like L. She wondered whether Rosa might have actually been the one to introduce L. to her friend in the first place. Maybe he was Rosa's contact, as mentioned in the diary.

As Margit drove the last stretch of road to the airport, she considered the possibility that L. might have become so greedy that he wasn't satisfied with the money he was already taking in. It was a big leap to go from embezzler and informer to paid assassin, but maybe L. was ruthless enough to do it. Maybe he had agreed to become one of the agents who carried out the "clearing murders" for the Germans. And maybe he was even responsible for the death of the two doctors. That could be the reason why Rosa Nørgaard had saved the newspaper clipping.

But it was obvious from the last paragraph in Sven Stenstrup's diary that someone in the group eventually caught on to what L. was up to. And then the group had a hard time convincing Gudrun Madsen of her lover's guilt.

Margit realized with a start that Gudrun, with her connections to the medical community, might have inadvertently given L. the idea for his choice of victims. If that was the case, her possible complicity in the murders might have made Gudrun even more loath to accept the truth about her lover.

But all of this was sheer speculation, and there were still plenty of unanswered questions. Margit had no idea who L. was or what had become of him. And she hadn't been able to figure out why events that happened in occupied Denmark would result in three deaths in Seattle more than half a century later.

And she still didn't know who was making those disturbing phone calls.

Margit entered the airport parking garage and began driving up the circular ramp. All the lower floors were full, and it took her ten minutes to find a spot on the seventh floor. By that time it was already 9:30, and she was definitely going to be late for Don Schmidt's pep talk.

"Damn," she said, as she pulled into the parking slot and stomped on the brake, bringing the Mazda to a halt with a lurch. The faxes slid off the passenger seat, and Margit impatiently leaned down to retrieve them. She was surprised to find Sven Stenstrup's diary lying on the floor too—face down with some of the pages bent underneath. It must have fallen out of the side pocket of her overnight bag when she tossed it onto the front seat.

Margit picked up the diary with a sigh, just imagining what Tristano was going to say about the cavalier way in which she handled important police evidence.

As she tried to bend back the crumpled pages of the water-damaged diary, she noticed the corner of something sticking out near the back of the book.

Margit pried apart two pages that she hadn't managed to separate before, and then pulled out an old black-and-white photograph. She reached up and snapped on the ceiling light in the car so she could see better.

The photo had several cracks in the emulsion but the image was as clear as the day the picture was taken.

Off to the right, five people were lounging around a table outdoors on a bright, sunny day, carrying on an animated conversation. The table was littered with dirty dishes, Carlsberg beer bottles, half-empty coffee cups, and all the other remnants of a long lunch. In the background on the left was a small summer house, and standing in the doorway with a tray in her hands was a laughing, young Rosa Nørgaard.

Feeling suddenly tense, Margit held the photo closer to the light. Then she studied the other people in the group.

"Oh my God," she gasped suddenly.

At the head of the table an attractive woman in her twenties, wearing a sleeveless dress, was sitting on a man's lap. Her left arm was draped around his neck, and her face was turned so she could look into her companion's eyes as she spoke. But even in profile Margit could clearly identify Gudrun Madsen.

The man had put his right arm around Gudrun's waist in a casually proprietary manner. In his left hand he held a cigarette. The camera had caught him staring straight into the lens, a faint smile on his lips and a slightly preoccupied look in his eyes, as if he weren't really paying attention to whatever Gudrun was telling him.

Margit was positive she was looking at a picture of L.

But what shocked her was that she had seen this man before. And she now knew exactly who he was.

21

Margit reached for the car phone to call the police. Her pulse was racing wildly as she dialed the number. Her face was flushed, her hands were clammy, and her throat was so tight that she barely recognized her own voice as she asked for the homicide department. Her call was transferred, and then the officer had to put her on hold so he could try to locate either Tristano or Silikov.

Margit stared at the photograph in her lap and nervously drummed the fingers of her left hand on the steering wheel as she waited. She was thinking about Rosa Nørgaard arriving at Sea-Tac on the previous Thursday, coming to meet two people she had once known well but might not have seen since the war. She must have been anxious and tense — judging from the note found in Gudrun Madsen's apartment, Rosa's visit was not entirely welcome.

Then, on her way down the escalator into the Immigration area after an exhausting nine-hour flight, Rosa suddenly caught sight of someone she had never expected to see. A man whose mere presence shattered her composure so completely that she began screaming and swinging her arms around. Terror seized hold of her mind, and she was only able to utter those last two coherent words, "Not him!" before her body succumbed to the overwhelming effects of fear.

All of a sudden a great roar erupted right behind Margit's car, followed by a sharp screech. She flinched violently and then whipped her head around to see what was going on.

But it was nothing—just some early morning hot-rodder backing out of a parking slot and showing off.

The ceiling light in her car was still on, and Margit suddenly realized how exposed she was, sitting there in the illuminated front seat. The sprawling concrete expanse of the parking garage was a gloomy place—dimly lit and nearly deserted. The only other people on the floor were at the far end of the building, hovering around the bank of elevators that would take them to one of the skybridges leading to the main terminal.

Margit slammed down the phone as panic overtook her. She wasn't going to stay in that place even one second longer. She switched off the ceiling light and turned the key in the ignition. An ugly grinding noise issued from the engine, and after three more attempts the car still refused to start. There was nothing to do but give up and head for the Star Air office.

Quickly Margit stuffed the photograph, faxes, and Sven Stenstrup's diary into her shoulder bag and then jumped out of the Mazda.

She ran past endless rows of parked cars and breathlessly skidded to a stop in front of an elevator just as the doors were closing. A matronly woman stuck her umbrella in the crack from inside and forced the doors back open.

"Come on, dear," she said briskly. "We wouldn't want you to miss your flight."

A few minutes later, Margit reached the ticketing level of the main terminal and entered the familiar hubbub of scurrying passengers. Her panic began to subside. The bright sunshine flooding the building through the enormous plate-glass windows made the whole setting seem so ordinary and safe. And Margit could feel the adrenaline ebbing away in her body as her pulse gradually returned to normal.

She slipped behind the Star Air ticket counter, pausing just long enough to wave hello to the agents who were busily checking in passengers.

As she went through the door into the airline office, Margit's only thought was to get to a phone. She had to tell the police about what she had discovered. And it was urgent. She headed straight for Brian's desk in the corner of the main room, but as she picked up the receiver, she realized with surprise that the place was almost empty.

"Where is everybody?" she asked Sharon, who was sitting at the cashier's table nearby, poring over a sales report.

"Oh, hi, Margit," said Sharon, looking up. "We were wondering what happened to you. Didn't you call the recording to check on the arrival time? The first flight's early today. In fact, it should be here in a few minutes. Brian and the rest of the arrival team already left for the South Satellite. He said you should meet them in Immigration."

"Just my luck," groaned Margit, putting the phone back down so she could rummage through her shoulder bag for her airline ID badge. She wouldn't be allowed into the secured areas of the airport without it.

"Having a bad day?" asked Sharon sympathetically.

"You have no idea," replied Margit, feeling thoroughly frazzled as she finally located her badge and pulled it out. Her silver Thor's hammer necklace was twisted around the metal clip. She had worn the pendant to the art opening she went to with Renny on Capitol Hill last Friday. In the course of an hour three different people had come up to Margit and said, "I like your whale necklace," and then proceeded to talk her ear off about the current whaling controversy. She finally decided that she'd heard enough about the topic for one night and slipped the necklace into her bag. Apparently some people thought a Thor's hammer looked a lot like the stylized image of a whale's flukes, as seen in Native American art on the Northwest coast.

Just then the cut channel began to sputter, and Sharon stood up to adjust the dial.

The squawking sounds solidified into comprehensible words, spoken with a lilting Norwegian accent.

"*God dag, god dag.* Captain Holm here. We'll need three wheelchairs for our passengers. And there's a mother with two youngsters who's going to need some assistance."

"Good morning, Captain. We've got the wheelchairs all lined up for you. And just tell the passenger who needs help to contact the ground staff in the jetway when she disembarks."

"Fine, fine. See you soon."

Sharon sat down and then noticed that Margit was still standing there. "You'd better run," she said, frowning. "The aircraft should be taxiing in at any moment."

"OK. I've just got to make a quick call—it'll only take a second."

Margit slid the Thor's hammer into her jacket pocket, clipped the ID badge to her lapel, and stuffed her bag under Brian's desk, out of sight. Then she hastily dialed the police again, but this time her call was transferred straight to Tristano's voice mail. Not wanting to give too many details with Sharon listening in, and feeling pressured for time, she simply said: "This is Margit. I read the diary and I found another old photograph. I'm out at the airport working for Star Air today. The flight's coming in right now, so I'll have to call you back later. But I'm pretty sure I know who did it."

Then she rushed out of the office and headed for the escalators that would take her downstairs to the subway level.

Unlike the multiple terminals at many other airports, the North and South Satellites at Sea-Tac were not directly connected to the main terminal. They had been constructed as separate, remote "pods" that couldn't be reached by bus or car or on foot. The only way to get to either satellite building was by subway, and each had its own subway loop and station at opposite ends of the airport.

Downstairs Margit found a huge crowd of German tourists clogging the security area, bantering and laughing as they piled their carry-on bags onto the conveyor belts to be screened. Looking beyond the checkpoint, she noted with dismay that the shiny steel doors to the subway had just opened to disgorge a swarm of arriving passengers. Then the people who had already been cleared through security eagerly pressed forward and stepped inside the two cars, bound for the South Satellite. At the last minute a portly man leaped on board, shouting, "*Ich komme mit!*" Then the doors closed and the subway train was gone.

It's just not my day, thought Margit with a sigh of resignation as she futilely tried to weave her way through the crowd toward the arch of the metal detector. At this rate, she was going to miss two or three more subways before she managed to get through. Airline flight crews were exempt from security procedures and could bypass the checkpoints; members of the ground staff could not. But if Margit ever got close enough to the front of the line, she would flash her ID badge to the security guard. Then she would be allowed to pass through ahead of everyone else.

At that moment her attention was caught by two loud and belligerent young men. They had obviously started off the morning with a few drinks, and somewhere along the way their boisterous mood had turned mean. Now they were shouting and swearing at each other, and suddenly fists began to fly. Everyone scattered to avoid getting hit—and that's when Margit saw him.

He was standing at the edge of the crowd some distance away, off to the left. His eyes were fixed on the snarling combatants, as he watched the fight with an expression of disdainful amusement. He was wearing the standard navy-blue uniform, but it didn't seem to fit him quite right. The jacket was baggy and the sleeves were a tad too short. The gold insignia on his uniform identified him as a pilot, but he seemed in no hurry to make use of his prerogative to circumvent the security checkpoint. His thinning white hair was neatly trimmed and slicked back from his high forehead. His gaunt face was creased and lined, and he seemed well beyond the retirement age for a commercial pilot. But there was a certain athletic vitality to his tall, lean frame, as if he worked hard to keep himself fit.

For a moment the anonymity of the uniform fooled Margit. But when the man abruptly glanced in her direction, she found herself staring into the same startling blue eyes that she had seen the day before. And she recognized him at once.

Her pulse surged, her throat clamped shut, and her heart went cold with dread. The family resemblance was astounding, in spite of an age difference of more than fifty years. There was no question that she was looking into the eyes of Ulf Hansson's grandfather.

But what scared her was that she was also looking into the eyes of the man known as L.

Back in the parking garage, when Margit had pulled the old photograph out of Sven Stenstrup's diary, she was shocked to discover Gudrun Madsen sitting on the lap of a man who was the spitting image of Ulf Hansson. Similar features and family traits often skipped a generation, and Margit was reminded of that picture of Renny's great-aunt, who could have been her twin.

In 1944 Ulf's grandfather would have been in his early twenties, and except for a different haircut and clothing, in that photo he looked exactly the way Ulf looked today.

As she sat in her car, trying to get hold of Detective Tristano, Margit had replayed in her mind everything that Ulf had told her at the Retrograde the day before.

She pictured Ulf standing against the glass of the Immigration viewing area a week ago as Rosa Nørgaard came down the escalator. She imagined how jolting it must have been for the old woman to see that unexpected face from her past, so untouched by the intervening years—his skin still youthful and firm, his eyes still alert and bright. It must have been a tremendous shock.

That would partially explain Rosa's extreme reaction. She was literally yanked back in time and confronted with a man who obviously evoked terrifying memories. Her mind had refused to assimilate what she was seeing, and the trauma was so great that her heart simply gave out.

Gudrun Madsen and Sven Stenstrup had been there that day too, and they must have watched with astonishment as Rosa collapsed.

Ulf had said: "My grandfather came over to the viewing area just then and asked me what was going on. I remember seeing the couple glance in our direction, and then they both took off fast."

Margit imagined the sense of stunned disbelief that Gudrun and Sven must have felt as they turned around to see Ulf standing next to his grandfather—the past and the present side by side. No wonder they panicked and took off at once. There was something about the sudden appearance of L. that frightened them so badly that they didn't want anyone to know about their connection with Rosa Nørgaard.

Now, surrounded by the crush of shouting and jostling people at the security checkpoint, Margit could understand their terror. She was convinced that the man standing less than thirty feet away was responsible for at least two recent murders, in addition to whatever unspeakable acts he might have committed in the past. And she was also certain that he was waiting there for her.

Margit spun on her heel and began desperately pushing and shoving her way back through the crowd. Curses and complaints rained down on her in both German and English, but she was oblivious to them all. Finally she reached the bottom of the steep escalator which led up to the baggage level of the main terminal. A quick glance over her shoulder revealed that L. was not far behind, struggling to get through the mob.

With a gasp, Margit raced up the steps, practically knocking over six or seven people who were blocking her way. "Sorry!" she managed to yell in reply to their angry protests, and then she reached the top of the escalator.

Several aircraft had obviously just arrived and the baggage

claim areas on both sides were noisy and chaotic, swarming with impatient passengers, excited family members, and busy skycaps. It would take Margit too long to fight her way through all those people to reach the doors opening onto the airport drive. The only clear route was straight ahead and up another escalator to a skybridge.

Margit scrambled up the stairs, but one glance toward the cavernous parking garage made her change her mind about heading for her car. There was no guarantee that she could even get it started, and with a shiver she imagined what would happen if L. caught up with her in that dim and deserted place.

She turned and dashed up the next flight of stairs to the ticketing level. She was halfway to a stand of telephones, planning to dial 911, when Margit heard a low voice behind her say in Swedish, "I've got a gun. Do what I say or I'm going to have to start shooting. If you don't believe me, just try screaming. But keep in mind that you won't be the only one to get hurt."

Margit froze. Her eyes were fixed on a little girl in a yellow sundress sitting in a stroller amidst a throng of people not more than ten feet away. Visions of the Rome airport massacre rose up before her. Even if L. only had a handgun, it would be enough to inflict serious injury on a number of people before he was stopped. And from the tone of his voice, Margit had no doubt that he *was* carrying some kind of weapon, and that he wouldn't hesitate to use it.

She would just have to pretend to cooperate and then look for an opportunity to escape.

Margit could feel the sweat trickling down her sides. Her heart was hammering, her pulse was racing, and her fingers were icy with fear. She took in a deep, shuddery breath and told herself to calm down. Panicking wasn't going to help matters. She looked over her shoulder at the stern face of the white-haired man standing behind her and felt sick to her stomach.

Keep him talking, she thought to herself. Buy yourself some time. So in Swedish she asked him the only thing that she could think of at the moment.

"Where'd you get the uniform?"

"Stole some guy's dry-cleaning out of his car. Now get moving. We'll take the next escalator on the right, down to the skybridge. But walk slowly and don't try anything stupid."

22

Despair descended on Margit as she reluctantly took the first few steps toward the escalator with her unwelcome companion right behind. She felt as if she were moving at an infinitely slow pace, pushing her way through a wall of hot, shimmering air. The crowds of people around her dissolved into a blur of unidentifiable shapes and colors. The words of their incessant chatter disintegrated into a buzz of white noise. And the loudspeaker announcements in the airport faded into an unintelligible drone. She was wrapped in a cocoon of paralyzing fear.

Off to the right a door abruptly slid open and a cool gust of wind blew straight into Margit's face before the entrance was filled with another amorphous swell of humanity.

And then something snapped inside her.

Defiantly Margit raised her chin and clenched her fists as she recalled one of her mother's favorite sayings: *Det er et sølle menneske, der ikke kan blive vred.* "It's a pathetic person who isn't capable of getting mad."

In a flash, everything around her came back into sharp

focus. Without turning her head, Margit began furiously scanning the terminal, looking for some way to divert her captor's attention so she could flee without endangering anyone else. The escalator to the skybridge wasn't far away, and she was going to have to stall for time. She decided to ask him more questions— maybe that would distract him enough to give her a chance to figure out what to do. But she didn't want to provoke him, so she started off with something relatively innocuous.

"How come you were hanging around the security checkpoint?" Margit asked in Swedish, trying to keep her voice steady. "Why didn't you catch the subway and wait for me in the South Satellite, where you'd be less conspicuous?"

"I don't have a flight crew ID, and I couldn't take the gun through security. But I figured you'd show up sooner or later to go out to meet the charter flights. And with the crowd of tourists making all that ruckus, nobody was paying any attention to me, anyway."

"I guess you saw me helping Rosa Nørgaard when she collapsed in Immigration last Thursday, didn't you? Is that why you've been calling my house all week?"

L. laughed harshly. "The airline wouldn't give out your address, but I found your number in the phone book. I just wanted to keep tabs on you and give you a little scare at the same time. But then my grandson told me about your conversation with him yesterday, and I decided you were getting too nosy for your own good."

Margit shivered at the dire implication of his words. Slowing her pace still further, she decided to change the subject.

"I read something that referred to you as L. What does that stand for, anyway? Did you have a code name during the war, like Gudrun and Sven?"

The man snorted scornfully. "Huginn and Muninn—those two and their games. When Rosa first contacted me about working with them, they were calling themselves the 'Odin group' because the man in charge had lost an eye, just like Odin. Everybody had some kind of mythological pseudonym, and they wanted to give me one too, but I didn't have time for such nonsense. I told them they could just call me Lennart, and they finally agreed. But Gudrun liked to tease me by calling me Loki, since I was good at disguises. It wasn't until later on that she found out how appropriate that name really was."

And this time his laugh sounded even more cruel.

"Did Rosa have a code name too?" Margit hurried to ask.

"They named her Freyja, but it never really stuck. She was much too mousy and plain to be the goddess of love. Everyone just called her Rosa. But I had my own nickname for her—it was our little secret. You might say it was sort of a joke between us, because of something that happened when we were kids. I always called her Idun."

Margit's eyes widened as she remembered what she had read about Idun in her mythology book. The goddess was mainly known as the guardian of the apples that kept the gods from growing old. But according to a skaldic poem, one day Idun was seized by the giants and raped. And her rescuer was none other than Loki. It was one of the few good deeds he had to his credit.

If something similar had actually happened to Rosa, maybe that's why she was initially blind to Lennart's true nature. Maybe that's why she trusted him enough to bring him into the group. But Rosa probably wouldn't have thought it much of a "joke" to be called Idun. If Margit was guessing right, the name must have been a constant reminder of a painful episode in Rosa's past.

Then Lennart grew impatient and stepped up to Margit's side. "Now quit talking and get moving," he growled. And he jabbed at her right arm with the hard muzzle of the gun that he was clutching in his jacket pocket.

The sound of a familiar shrill voice suddenly caught Margit's ear. She glanced to her left and saw Elinor Bristol, the maven of airport PR, making a beeline for the very same escalator. She was gesturing vigorously and talking a mile a minute to a large group of teenage Explorer Scouts dutifully trying to keep up with her. She was a transplanted New Yorker who had never relinquished her aggressive manner or flamboyant style. Today she was dressed in an orange silk suit, and her three-inch heels were clicking feverishly against the concrete floor as she led the group on one of her popular tours.

Margit had met Elinor only a few weeks back when she took one of the airport tours as part of her job orientation. Elinor professed to be thrilled to meet an interpreter, exclaiming with amazement, "I don't know how you do it. I'm just no good at foreign languages myself." She seemed to take a special interest in Margit, and she had fired off a battery of questions about translation work.

Now Elinor waved merrily and called "Hello" as she briskly ushered her group past.

That's when Margit made up her mind.

Abruptly she stuck out her left arm and grabbed the tour guide's silk sleeve.

"Elinor!" she cried. "Wouldn't the boys like to talk to a real pilot?"

"Oh my, yes. What a great idea, Margit!" shrieked Elinor with delight, as she spied the tall, white-haired man in the airline uniform. "Come on boys, gather round." And she instantly hustled the group into a tight little knot around Lennart.

194

As Margit slipped away and took off running, she fleetingly registered the look of surprise and anger that flooded Lennart's face as he found himself so unexpectedly surrounded. But there was no time to waste. Even Elinor's bulldozer-like charm wasn't going to be able to hold him for long.

Margit raced past the crowded ticket counters, deciding instinctively to keep going instead of trying to enlist the aid of one of the harried airline agents. Even if she managed to force her way through all the people, it would take too long to explain why she needed the police. The ticket agents would probably just assume that she was another stressed-out passenger, trying to skip ahead in line—especially since she seemed to have lost her ID badge on her mad dash up the escalators from the subway level.

Above the din of the terminal, Margit suddenly thought she could hear someone calling her name. She ran even faster.

Out of the corner of her eye, she saw a wide opening between the counters, and she automatically veered toward it. A few seconds later Margit found herself in the so-called "central plaza" of the airport.

The courtyard setting was nearly deserted, as usual, since the main passenger thoroughfares went around it rather than through it. On the left, an open stairway led up to a kind of long balcony or gallery, overlooking the plaza. On either side of the balcony, narrow corridors meandered along the mezzanine level, where a few obscure administrative offices were located. Except for the occasional employee in need of a parking permit or a mournful agent in search of the chaplaincy, few people ever had business that took them along the balcony.

But Margit had been to this part of the airport before because Joe wanted to show her the huge jutting contours of a sculpture by Robert Maki, which dominated the plaza. She remembered him giving her an enthusiastic lecture about the artist and the "muscular force" of his work. But to her, the matte-black surfaces and sharp edges of the two irregular shapes looked like a cross between Darth Vader and a stealth bomber—although the sculpture predated both.

Out of breath, Margit paused just long enough to cast a fearful glance over her shoulder. A few sullen-looking passengers hurried past, lugging their bags behind them. Then they vanished from view, and the plaza was once again empty.

But at that moment Lennart appeared from around the corner, sliding to a stop to survey the scene. He spotted her at once.

Margit raced up the steps, taking them two at a time.

When she reached the top, she turned right and ran along the balcony, past a series of display cases holding artwork from a famous glass-blowing studio.

At the far end of the balcony was the Meditation Room, a self-contained island of space surrounded by corridors on all four sides. Off to the right was a door to one of the airport offices. That's where Margit was headed.

All she wanted was someone with authority who had a phone or a radio within easy reach. She figured she would shout "Get the police!" as she dashed inside the office, slamming the door shut behind her and praying for a fast reaction from whoever was on duty.

She could hear Lennart's feet pounding along the balcony—she didn't have much of a lead.

But when Margit reached the office, gasping for air, she found the door inexplicably locked with a little card taped to the door frame. "Back in ten minutes," it said.

"No!" she protested, slamming her hand against the wood.

And then he was standing right behind her.

"*Satans tös*," hissed Lennart as he jammed the gun hard into Margit's back. But the sound of loud voices fast approaching in the hallway apparently made him change his mind about shooting her on the spot.

"In there," he commanded, giving Margit a shove toward the nearby Meditation Room. She had no choice but to pull open the door, and then they both stepped inside.

She couldn't have ended up in a worse place. Brian had once told Margit that whenever he was in need of a few minutes of solitude to regain his sanity on an especially hectic day, he would retreat to the Meditation Room. In the eight years he had worked at the airport he had seldom encountered anyone else inside.

The glass door opened onto a tiny foyer, which was separated from the room by a floor-to-ceiling partition, with an entryway on either side. The room itself was rather like a chapel, with soft carpeting and subdued lighting. Five rows of chairs were lined up in front of a wooden table set against the far wall. Above the table hung a spotlighted painting of a lake at sunset, with the surrounding mountains silhouetted against a warm orange sky. Tall narrow windows at each corner of the room were covered with weavings, which prevented any clear view of the interior from the outside corridors. The place had been carefully designed to encourage privacy and self-reflection. The silence was palpable.

Margit was terrified but also furious. She was angry at Rosa and Gudrun and Sven for getting her tangled up in their story in the first place. And she was angry at herself for ignoring her own instincts. If she'd had any sense, she would have stayed away from the airport altogether.

But it was Lennart's arrogant assumption of power over all their lives that enraged Margit the most. Hatred welled up inside her, overshadowing everything else. She stuffed her fists into her jacket pockets, and the fingers of her right hand closed around the familiar shape of her silver Thor's hammer. It seemed to give her courage as she turned around to face the man holding the gun.

"Why are you doing this?" she demanded to know. "Why did you kill Gudrun and Sven? Are you still holding a grudge after all these years, just because of some minor quarrel during the war?"

"Minor quarrel!" spat Lennart, his eyes narrowing. "You have no idea what you're talking about. They all conspired against me."

"What do you mean?"

"I was supposed to take some refugees across to Sweden one night. But when I got to the meeting place on the shore, I found Rosa and her two 'raven' friends waiting there for me. They accused me of being an embezzler and an informer."

"And were you?"

"Well, yes. As a matter of fact, I was," said Lennart with a nasty smile.

"And did you also murder those Copenhagen doctors? On that night in July of 1944?" Margit asked, her voice cold with loathing.

"How the hell did you find out about that? I can't believe Rosa would talk about it, since she was in on it too."

"What do you mean she was in on it?"

"I told her that I'd tracked down the man who had raped her when she was twelve—that he was living in Denmark now and that he was working with the Germans against the resistance. Of course it wasn't true, but she believed me. I gave her a gun and showed her how to use it, and then I sent her off to kill one of those doctors."

"Why?"

"I figured that if she actually went through with it, I'd have an even bigger hold on her than before. I already had Gudrun on my side, but I needed another ally in the group. Sven was getting suspicious about my activities, and he was starting to make things unpleasant for me. I hadn't counted on him being such a damn good bookkeeper."

Lennart frowned and shook his head.

"Did Rosa really kill one of the doctors?" Margit asked. She found it hard to imagine the distraught old woman at the airport harboring such a violent deed in her past. She thought of the two photos she had seen of Rosa: the girl in the old-fashioned bathing suit, sitting on the beach with her friend Gudrun. And the laughing young woman standing in the doorway of the summer house. But by that time Rosa already had one hideous secret gnawing at her soul, and the war had turned the whole world upside down. Ordinary people were driven to extreme measures. And Lennart was clearly in a position to manipulate Rosa's emotions.

"She shot him, all right. She was a lot tougher than I thought," said Lennart, with a hint of admiration in his voice.

"Who killed the other doctor?"

"I did. I wasn't sure that Rosa was going to pull it off, and I had a contract to fulfill. So I went after the other doctor myself, just in case. I ended up collecting a double fee for my services. It was a very profitable night."

Margit shuddered, but she was determined to keep Lennart talking for as long as she could. He seemed almost eager to tell her what had happened—as if the words had been bottled up inside him for the past fifty years, and at long last he had the opportunity to gloat. And now that he had her safely cornered, he was confident that his words would never leave the room.

"Was it Gudrun who gave you the idea to choose the doctors?"

"Sweet Gudrun," said Lennart with a leer. "She turned out to be very useful, in more ways than one. You know, deep down she could never really believe all those things that Sven and Rosa told her about me. She went along with the group's decision, but apparently she's been carrying a torch for me all these years. When she got over the shock of seeing me again, she was actually relieved to find out that I didn't die on that Danish beach, after all. She was even foolish enough to let me into her apartment."

Margit remembered Detective Silikov mentioning that the deadbolt wasn't fastened in Gudrun Madsen's apartment.

"What do you mean by you 'didn't die on that Danish beach'?"

"The group had decided to execute me for my sins," said Lennart derisively. "Rosa volunteered to do it, since she'd found out that I'd tricked her into killing an innocent man. And the others didn't really have the stomach for cold-blooded murder. But lucky for me, Rosa botched the job and shot me in the chest instead of the head."

"Then what happened?"

"They left me there to die. But a German patrol boat found me, and I managed to explain who I was. I ended up in a hospital in Lübeck, but it took almost a year for me to get back on my feet."

The memory made Lennart's face darken with anger, and

Margit was appalled to see his fingers tighten their grip on the gun.

She rushed to change the subject, hoping to divert his attention to less dangerous thoughts. "Your grandson told me that you've been living in Germany," she said rather inanely.

"Berlin," he replied, his voice icy. "East Berlin."

And Margit could see that she had badly miscalculated. This was not a topic that she should have brought up.

"That's enough questions," said Lennart harshly. "You've run out of time." Then he smiled and resolutely raised his gun higher to take aim.

At that moment the door on the other side of the partition creaked open.

For a split second Lennart took his eyes off Margit and glanced to the left.

Instantly Margit leaped to the side, out of the line of fire. At the same moment she pulled her hand out of her pocket, thrust out her arm, and lunged for Lennart's face. With all her might she jabbed the sharp corner of the Thor's hammer right into his eye. It sank deep into the soft tissue, making a vicious wound.

Lennart clapped his free hand to his face with a gruesome howl. The searing pain blinded him and bent him double. Bellowing with rage, he began firing wildly around the room.

Bullets ricocheted off the wall, and one of them grazed Margit's arm as she frantically scrambled to get past Lennart's writhing form. Her heart was hammering in her chest, her blood was roaring in her ears, and she was dimly aware that she was screaming.

Margit darted around the partition, threw herself against the half-open door, and then bolted along the balcony overlooking the plaza. Ahead of her she could see an airline agent madly racing down the far corridor, obviously panic-stricken by the violent response that had erupted when she unsuspectingly opened the door to the Meditation Room.

Footsteps suddenly thundered behind Margit. Shots rang out. Something whistled past her cheek. A glass display case shattered. She crouched low and kept on running.

Shots caromed all around her, seeming to come from more than one direction. But when Margit reached the top of the stairway, she heard a horrifying shriek behind her. And then for a long moment the only sound was her own ragged breathing. In a daze, she turned around and saw Lennart collapsed in a heap on the balcony.

Then people started pouring into the plaza, yelling and screaming. Police officers appeared out of nowhere, and Margit thought she heard someone shouting her name from below. Numbly, she looked down and saw Detective Tristano making his way through the crowd. She noticed that he had a gun in his hand, which he turned over to one of the officers before he began sprinting up the stairs.

"What are you doing here?" she called out as he approached.

"I got your phone message, and I rushed over here as fast as I could."

Tristano had to shout to be heard over the commotion both on the balcony and in the plaza below.

"I saw you racing through the terminal," he continued. "And I knew something was up, but then you disappeared into the crowd. Didn't you hear me calling your name?"

Margit shook her head.

"Did you shoot him?" she asked as the detective finally reached her side.

"Yes, I did."

Then he glanced down and noticed the blood seeping out of her sleeve and trickling onto the floor.

"Margit," he said, his voice full of concern. "Are you all right?"

She nodded, tried to speak, but couldn't say another word.

Then Tristano stepped over to Margit and took her in his arms.

Epilogue

Saturday turned out to be another brilliantly sunny day, and the weather forecasters were predicting a record high of 95 degrees.

Margit was up early.

As she stepped out the back door to feed the birds and the squirrels, she called "Good morning" to her neighbor, Mr. Nettlebury. He was just returning home from his night-shift job at a local convenience store, and he came over to find out how she was doing.

"I know you don't like to read the news," he said, "but I brought you a copy of this morning's paper anyway. There's another story on page 4." He put the newspaper on the patio table in Margit's yard. Then he said kindly, "Take care." And with a wave he shambled off to make himself a light meal and watch TV for a couple of hours before going to bed.

Margit wasn't quite ready to read another sensationalized account of what the media had promptly dubbed the "Raven

Murders." The story had been front page news on Thursday night. And now, two days later, it was still getting attention on the local TV stations. Margit's father had called to tell her that even CNN had reported the story.

But right now she just wanted to take it easy and enjoy the morning while it was still cool enough to be outdoors. She would look at the newspaper later on, after she had another cup of coffee.

Margit walked over to the Scotch pine and lifted the top of the bird feeder with her left hand. Then she bent down to pick up the glass measuring cup from the ground where she had set it. Awkwardly she poured the millet and sunflower seeds into the bird feeder, spilling an equal amount onto the grass below.

Gregor leaped out of range with a plaintive meow and then sat down a few feet away to keep an eye on Margit.

Her right arm was bandaged and strapped into a sling. The emergency room doctor had pronounced the bullet wound "superficial," but it was still painful and throbbing. She sank into one of the lawn chairs with a sigh, closed her eyes, and lifted her face to the sun. She was thinking about all the people who had called her the day before.

The shock of the whole airport episode on Thursday had left Margit completely drained. After her arm was patched up and she was found fit enough to answer questions, she went through a lengthy interview with the police. They were anxious to put together the final pieces in this unusual case, which had ended up involving four deaths. The alleged murderer, whom Margit knew only as Lennart, had died of gunshot wounds on the way to the hospital from the airport.

A brief press conference with a dozen frenzied reporters on

Thursday evening had taken Margit's last ounce of strength. She spent most of Friday at home, stretched out on the sofa, pretending to read.

The phone had rung nonstop, but for once she actually welcomed the constant interruptions. She wasn't in the middle of a translation job, after all—in fact, she had told Liisa that she was taking a week off. And after her traumatic experience at the airport, Margit had a great craving for ordinary human conversation. Instead of unplugging the phone, she just moved it over to the coffee table, within reach of her left hand.

Egon Kirkeby was one of the first people to call.

"I've been reading about the whole story in the *Times*," he said excitedly in Danish. "So you were right all along—the murders here in Seattle *did* have something to do with the Øresund routes."

"Yes," said Margit. "And I don't think I ever thanked you properly for all your help. You were the one who started me off thinking in the right direction."

"The paper says the motive for the murders was revenge."

"I know," replied Margit, thinking about what Egon had told her only a few days earlier, although it now seemed like ages ago. He had been talking about the type of people who committed acts of treachery out of greed or the lust for power. And she remembered him saying: "If you cross them, they're not the kind who would ever forgive... or forget."

Margit shivered and then shook her head, as if to erase from her mind the memory of Lennart's angry face.

"By the way," she said to Egon on the phone, "I gave the police your name and number, in case they needed more information about the Danish resistance or the route networks."

"Yes, I know. A Detective Tristano came by the house yesterday to ask me a few questions. A very nice young man. Most polite."

Margit couldn't help smiling at the mention of the detective's name. Her heart skipped a beat, and she could feel the heat rising in her face. Don't get distracted, she scolded herself as she swung her legs down from the sofa and sat up. The movement prompted a stab of pain in her right arm, and she winced as she tried to concentrate on what Egon was saying.

"We were sitting in the living room, talking about the case, when my father suddenly chimed in. You know how certain words or phrases can sometimes jog his memory? Well, when he heard the detective mention the 'Odin group,' he suddenly started in on a rambling account about one of his friends named Henrik who escaped to Sweden in the summer of 1944. Apparently there was something fishy about his finances, so Henrik didn't want to go through the big refugee organizations to get his savings out of Denmark. Instead he ended up contacting a small freelance outfit with connections in Hälsingborg. It was known as the Odin group."

"Then what happened?" asked Margit with interest.

"They brought his money over to Sweden, all right, but my father said that when Henrik finally received the funds, he discovered that double the normal fee had been deducted. When he went back to his contacts in Hälsingborg to complain, they told him he was out of luck because the group had suddenly disbanded."

"Did your father know why?"

"No, that's all he could tell us. He repeated the same story twice and then fell asleep while I was translating what he said for the detective. But most of those freelance groups didn't operate for long. It was common for new ones to sprout up every few months or so and then disappear overnight. And if the newspaper story is right and the members of the Odin group were involved in the disappearance of a Nazi collaborator, then it's no wonder the group split up. It would have been too risky for them to keep working together, running boats across Øresund."

"Why do you think Rosa Nørgaard decided all of a sudden to come over here?" Margit then asked Egon. "Why do you think she wanted to see Gudrun and Sven again?"

This was one issue that still had the authorities puzzled.

"I don't really know, but there are plenty of people who have never been able to put the war behind them. Especially if they were forced to do certain things that were necessary under the circumstances—but that in normal times would be considered morally wrong."

"Such as killing somebody? Even if it was justified because that person turned out to be a dangerous informer?"

"Exactly. Over time, most people managed to find a way to reconcile themselves to what had happened during the war, so they could get on with their lives. But some people ended up with their psyches permanently damaged, and those are the ones who will always feel haunted. It's possible that after all these years Rosa Nørgaard couldn't stand the burden of her past anymore. Maybe she needed to talk to somebody who shared her secret memories. That might be why she came to Seattle to see Gudrun and Sven."

"You could be right," said Margit, and she had the distinct impression that Egon knew from personal experience about wrestling with specters from the past.

As soon as she hung up the phone, it started ringing again.

This time it was the Star Air station manager, Don Schmidt, who asked in a booming voice, "How's my interpreter girl doing?"

For once the phrase actually made Margit smile, because she could hear that it was meant affectionately.

"I'm doing fine," she told him. "Thanks for asking."

"Well, OK. Good," he said, sounding a little embarrassed by his own feelings. "I want to see you back on the team next week. Now here's Brian."

"My God, Margit. How are you?" exclaimed Brian anxiously on the phone. "I feel terrible about getting you involved in this whole thing."

"Hey, it's not your fault. Who could have known something like this would happen just from helping out a distressed passenger?"

Then Margit changed the subject, and it was a relief to talk about other matters for a few minutes. It made her feel almost normal again. And Brian couldn't resist telling Margit that he had just sold a short story to a prominent West Coast journal. A story he wrote himself—not a translation.

"Great," said Margit, "I didn't know you were doing your own writing. I can't wait to read it." She was thrilled that her friend was finally making use of his literary talents again.

The next phone call was from her colleague, Lars. He told her that he had spent Thursday night assisting the police by translating various items in German and Swedish that had been found among the murderer's effects.

"They still can't figure out whether Lennart was his real name or not," Lars told Margit. "He had a German passport issued under the name of Gustav Schenk, and that's what his family called him. He always claimed that his mother was Swedish but his father was German, and that's why he could speak both languages fluently. But the police now suspect that he must have assumed his German identity after he got out of the hospital in Lübeck. Things were so chaotic back then that it would have been easy to step into the shoes of someone who had died or disappeared."

"Why would he stay in Germany after the war was over?"

"He probably figured it was a safer bet to start a new life as a German citizen instead of returning to Scandinavia where the authorities might start looking into what he'd been up to. The penalties for collaboration could be quite unpleasant, to say the least."

"Lennart told me that he was from East Berlin," said Margit, recalling the icy sound of the man's voice as he spoke those words.

"That's right. The police are still trying to unravel the whole story, but apparently he got caught on the wrong side of the Wall when it went up in 1961. His wife and daughter were able to escape to Sweden, but Lennart never managed to get out. His wife died shortly afterwards, and his daughter emigrated to Seattle in 1974 when she married a Swedish-American engineer named August Hansson. Ulf Hansson is their son."

Margit shook back her hair, not sure that she was keeping all the family relationships straight.

"It's strange how things turn out," she mused. "Lennart escaped death on the Danish beach, but then he ended up a virtual prisoner in Germany for almost thirty years. He must have blamed the Odin group for that too. And I wonder if the cash that was found in Rosa's safe-deposit box actually belonged to Lennart. Maybe it was the blood money he earned from the Nazis. But if he was so set on revenge, I wonder why he didn't track down the members of the group before. He must have been able to travel freely before the Wall finally trapped him in East Germany for good."

"Uh-huh. The police asked Lennart's family about that, and his daughter remembered that he had made several trips north during the fifties, when she was a child. But by then Gudrun and Sven had left for the U.S., and Rosa had married a Dane and changed her last name. Maybe she had also cut off all ties with her family and former friends, the way Gudrun evidently had. Maybe Lennart tried to find them before but without success."

"So it was just a coincidence that he came to Seattle to visit his family right now?"

"Apparently that's true. His daughter said she's been trying to get him to come over here for several years, and he finally agreed. He arrived a few weeks ago, and last Thursday he just happened to drive out to the airport with his grandson Ulf to pick up another family member coming for a visit."

There was a long pause as Margit and Lars both considered the peculiar convergence of events that had brought Rosa, Gudrun, Sven, and Lennart to exactly the same place at the same moment—more than fifty years after they had last met. And with such fateful consequences for them all.

Then Lars continued, "By the way, the police found another one of those old copper coins in Lennart's suitcase. The one you told me about that says: 'The walls have ears.'"

As Margit hung up the phone, she thought about what an unlikely talisman that coin was for Lennart to be carrying around all this time. It was meant as a warning about the presence of an informer, like himself—but maybe he kept it as a reminder that he had unfinished business with his past. And the police now assumed that Lennart was the one who had left the other coin next to Gudrun Madsen's body—a taunting gesture that had eventually led to his undoing.

A sharp meow from Gregor brought Margit back to the present. She opened her eyes and blinked at the bright sun. The phone was ringing in the house again. She scrambled to her feet and hurried inside to answer it, since she had purposely turned off her answering machine. Gregor trotted along behind her.

"Hi, kiddo," said Renny warmly when Margit picked up the receiver. "How's it going? Are you feeling better today?"

"Yes, much better," said Margit, as she perched on the arm of the sofa.

Renny had stopped by on Thursday evening to check up on her friend, and yesterday she had brought over a sumptuous lunch from the Cedar Café. Now she wanted to know if anything new had been uncovered in the investigation, and Margit obligingly told her the latest details.

As they talked, Margit could hear music coming from her study. She must have left the CD player on when she went out to feed the birds. She suddenly recognized the familiar melody—it was the Doobies singing "Is Love Enough?"

Then she missed what Renny was saying on the phone and had to ask her to repeat it.

"I just wanted to know if you feel up to coming to my opening at the gallery tonight," said Renny.

"Of course. I can't wait to see the show. And besides, it'll do me good to get out of the house."

At that moment someone knocked on the front door, and Margit told Renny, "Hold on a sec—I'll be right back."

She put down the phone, walked across the living room, and pulled open the door.

Detective Tristano was standing on the porch.

"Off-duty today?" asked Margit as soon as she saw him, and she couldn't help smiling at his uncharacteristic attire. For once he had traded in his suit for a pair of shorts, Nikes, and a t-shirt from the Monterey jazz festival.

"I've got the weekend off," said the detective, brusquely, looking a little nervous. "I just stopped by to see if you'd like to take a drive up to Whidbey Island. I thought you might want to get out of the city on such a hot day. And I know a good restaurant for lunch."

"That would be fun," said Margit, flushing with pleasure. "It'll take me a few minutes to get ready. Come on in and sit down. I'm just talking to a friend on the phone."

Tristano sat down in the armchair in the corner and looked around the room with interest. Gregor planted himself a few feet away and stared. Margit went back to the sofa and picked up the phone.

"Renny?" she said. "I've got to go now. But is it OK if I bring a guest to the opening tonight?"

"Sure. Who is it? Anyone I know?"

"Well, you two haven't actually met, but I think you know who he is," said Margit, glancing at the dark-haired man smiling at her from across the room. "His name is Alex."

Acknowledgments

I am indebted to the authors of the following reference works for both information and inspiration. All of these books are from the impressive Scandinavian collection in Suzzallo Library at the University of Washington. Any factual errors or misunderstandings that may have found their way into the story are, of course, my own.

De illegale Sverigesruter 1943–45. Studier i den maritime modstands historie, Henrik Dethlefsen (Odense: Odense Universitetsforlag, 1993)

Besættelsen og frihedskampen 1940–45. Hvem Hvad Hvor, ed. Jørgen Hæstrup, Hans Kirchhoff, Henning Poulsen & Hjalmar Petersen, 3rd edition (Copenhagen: Politikens Forlag, 1993)

De fem lange Aar. Danmark under Besættelsen 1940–45, Johannes Brøndsted & Knud Gedde (Copenhagen: Gyldendal, 1946)

Danmarks historie, Vol. 14: *Besættelse og Atomtid, 1939–1978*, Frantz Wendt (Copenhagen: Politikens Forlag, 1978)

About the Author

Tiina Nunnally is known for her award-winning translations of novels and short stories from Danish, Norwegian, and Swedish. Before becoming a freelance translator and writer, she spent ten years working on the "front lines" for an international airline. The author lives in Seattle with her editor husband Steve and their calico cat Amalie.

Other selected fiction from Fjord Press

Love Like Gumbo
by Nancy Rawles
$14.00 paperback

Nelio
A Novel of Mozambique
by Henning Mankell
Translated by Tiina Nunnally
$14.00 paperback

The Five Thousand and One Nights
by Penelope Lively
$12.00 paperback

Plenty Good Room
by Teresa McClain-Watson
$14.00 paperback

Runemaker
A Margit Andersson Mystery
by Tiina Nunnally
$12.00 paperback

Niels Lyhne
by Jens Peter Jacobsen
Translated by Tiina Nunnally
$14.00 paperback

Please write, fax, or email for a free catalog:
Fjord Press, PO Box 16349, Seattle, WA 98116
fax (206) 938-1991 / email fjord@halcyon.com
Visit our web site at www.fjordpress.com/fjord
for more information and reading samples